DEATH WAITS AT DAKINS STATION

DEATH WAITS AT DAKINS STATION

Merle Constiner

GUNSMOKE

First published in the US by Ace Books

This hardback edition 2012
by AudioGO Ltd
by arrangement with
Golden West Literary Agency

ISBN 978 1 445 82420 8

British Library Cataloguing in Publication Data available.

Printed and bound in Great Britain by
MPG Books Group Limited

I

A moist splattering of sleet was blowing that night, though autumn had scarcely started and the air was more wet that cold. Brady Willet, his wadded bandanna stuffed into the collar of his sleazy range shirt, stood on the dirt walk in the windowlight of the saloon behind him—the single saloon in this backcountry village—and thought, *Well, maybe tomorrow will be dry and sunny, hot even. Who knows?* Willet was young, shabby, frail-looking but rawhide tough. He was somewhere in north-central Montana, he knew, not far from the Little Belt Mountains. Here, as down in Wyoming where he had last worked, the cattle had been long shipped. He had been paid off at the chutes there, with most of the other hands, as was the custom, while the boss returned to his spread with a skeleton winter crew. All cowhands had fierce pride, and these

1

were the bad days for the out-of-workers, the hungry days, the humiliating days.

Willet's mare was tied to a post a few feet away. He was staring at her when a second horse appeared beside her out of the blackness of the early night, and a man slipped down from his saddle and came forward. He was tall and skinny, but for his belly which protruded melonlike, and wore a doeskin tunic with a long fringe encircling his shoulders.

He said gruffly, "You a gun tramp, son?"

"No," said Willet. It wasn't a compliment, and he put his feeling into his voice.

"I don't have no business with gun tramps," said the man.

"Sometimes you don't have no say-so," said Willet. He was thinking of some lean times, some hard days when he had almost gone on the gun himself.

"What trade *do* you follow?" asked the man.

"Cows and horses. Solely."

"You working now?"

"I don't much care for questions."

"Could be I'm fixing to offer you a job."

"No," said Willet. "I'm not working now."

After a steady minute, Willet said, "You make me nervous. I last worked down in Wyoming, outside of Cheyenne, on the Chugwater. For a man named Sorenson, brand *S Reversed.*"

"I know it," said the man, appearing satisfied. "That your horse?"

"Yes."

"Where you heading?"

2

"I don't know," said Willet. "Canada, maybe."

"Fine," said the man. "This won't be out of your way. You'll be taking the old mule wagon trail north for a spell. Two hours' ride from here you'll come to a couple of sorry-looking run-down buildings on your left. That's Dakins Station. It's been long out of use, and nobody's lived there for years. In the old days, it was a freighters' supply stage. Now it's weeds, mainly. and undergrowth. Rein up and call out, 'Mr. Lustrell!' Mr. Lustrell will come out, and you tell him Shaw can't make it. *Shaw can't make it.* Tell him I promised you ten dollars to carry the message. Then you take your ten dollars, bid him good night, and be on your way to Canada."

"Who are you?" asked Willet.

"That-there doesn't come into it. He'll know."

"Shouldn't I say something like, 'Terrible night, sir,' first? To make it more polite?"

"Suit yourself."

"Well, what about it? I'd like your opinion."

"Let's don't go splitting hairs."

"Who is this Mr. Lustrell?"

"A stockman, from due north of the old station. Owns most of that country, up on the edge of the Little Belts."

"Rich, Hey?"

"Poor. Land poor. Not as poor as you, but almost as poor as me."

"I've seen 'em like that down in Texas, hard

3

working ones, too," said Willet. "If they had a cow for every acre they'd be billionaires. What will he be doing there at that hour?"

"He'll be there to meet Shaw. And take him back with him."

The sleet was now pelting. Willet shifted his feet, canted his head, and said, "What if this Mr. Lustrell doesn't pay me?"

"He will. I said he would, didn't I? Stop quibbling. I'm a man of short temper."

Willet had thirty-five cents in his pocket, and five stale rock-hard cinnamon rolls in his saddlebags. The lean days were almost here. He said, "Who is Shaw?"

"That's none of your affair."

"Maybe you're Shaw?" said Willet.

"No, I'm not."

Suddenly the sleet stopped, and went into a miserable drizzle. Willet said, "What happened to Shaw that he can't make it?"

"Are you taking this job, or not?"

"I've always been sizable curious. And, besides, this Mr. Lustrell is going to ask."

"He got himself backshot, in the way of pleasure, by a derringer, in a parlor house in Fargo."

Willet smiled faintly. He said, "Somehow I get the feeling this is all going to be bad news for Mr. Lustrell."

The man in doeskin nodded.

"And he'll fork over ten dollars for bad news?" said Willet.

"Yes. He's got to know."

"I'll do it," said Willet.

He walked past the man, unhitched, mounted, and rode away at a lope.

At the edge of the village, the big road, which had been the village street, curved abruptly to the east; but the old mule road, mentioned by the man in doeskin, half discernible in the lamplight of the last house, continued due north, partly overgrown with fetlock-high oak seedlings and knobby with hummocks of long, dead grass. When the glow of the tiny village was behind him, he was engulfed in a wet muffling blackness. He went loose on the reins, loose on the bit, and left it entirely up to his stringy surefooted little mare. She'd forgotten more about night-trails than he'd ever know.

The temperamental autumnal weather changed. The mist and drizzle vanished as though they had been sucked away, there was a cool, damp, clean feeling inside his nostrils, and overhead the cloud layer went into sooty patches. Cobalt showed beyond, and grew, and the sky cleared. A moon appeared. The country on either side of the track became dimly visible. It looked to Willet like the rolling swales of sheep country.

The stars said nearly midnight when he came to the buildings on his left.

There were two of them, one set up to the edge of the track itself, and a second at its rear, at right angles—once stables probably—making a kind of broken-linked L.

5

They were sinister-looking and silent, dilapidated and dark. He studied them in the faint moonglow. There was no sign of man or beast.

He walked his mount from the track into the crotch of the L, relaxed in his saddle, thought, *What a wonderful spot for a crossfire,* and called, "Mr. Lustrell!"

A light appeared in the front building, through the grimy window and cracks in the clapboards, and a man came out and toward him carrying a candle. He wore a bulky sheepskin jacket, a flat crowned stockman's hat, and baggy corduroy breeches, cuffs inside his short black boots. The candle was in his left hand. In his right hand was a wicked looking .45 at full cock. Willet asked, "You Mr. Lustrell?"

"Yes," said the man. "Get down."

Willet swung to the ground. He said, "Mr. Lustrell, a man back in town—a man in a doeskin hunting-shirt—give me a message for you. You was to pay me ten dollars for toting it."

"Then let's have it."

"I can't do business that way," said Willet. "I got to have my ten dollars."

Lustrell handed him a ten dollar goldpiece.

Willet said, "Shaw can't make it. He got himself killed in a bawdy house in Fargo."

Lustrell said, "Don't move," and took Willet's gun.

On the ground, not far from where they stood, was a flat squarish rock. Lustrell shoved it aside with his foot. It had been covering a small oblong opening. It was a rainwater cistern that had been dug probably when the station had been built. Lustrell dropped Willet's gun in the hole—there was a hollow splash—and recovered the opening. "Now why in the hell did you do that?" Willet asked.

Lustrell said, "Now I'll take back that ten dollars."

Willet returned it.

Lustrell held the candle to Willet's face and gave it a close scrutiny. "You're a heap younger than I expected, Mr. Shaw."

"I ain't Shaw. I'm Brady Willet. Shaw got killed midst dalliance in Fargo. He can't come."

Lustrell, still gazing at him, shook his head. "They say you've slew a dozen men, Mr. Shaw. Is that true?"

"Yes," said Willet. "And just getting started. You owe me a gun and ten dollars."

"This man in doeskin," said Lustrell. "He was waiting for you?"

"No. He just happened to take notice of me in passing, and got down and spoke to me."

"Did you catch his name?"

"He didn't give it," said Willet. "I guess he figured you'd know."

"I do," said Lustrell. "Now just stand there straight, Mr. Shaw, shoulders back, chest out, hands down to your pants seams. Like you was honoring the raising of the colors at a army post."

7

He leveled his .45 and held it out target practice style.

"Why, you're fixing to kill me," said Willet, stunned.

"I sure am," said Lustrell. He seemed to be enjoying himself.

"You're going to shoot me like I was an empty beer bottle on a fencepost."

"Right."

Willet's little mare, catching a scent, whickered.

A neigh from within the stable, and a third horse, also from the stable, blew out a whinny.

The trio in the silent night startled Lustrell.

For the briefest of instants, his eyes flicked. Willet was on him in a lunge, right hand twisting Lustrell's gunwrist, left arm clenching his waist. They rocked back and forth in a sort of death embrace, Willet trying to force the weapon around and back, Lustrell, heavy muscled, fighting to bring it again to the fore. It was in this swaying, the gun momentarily behind Lustrell, when the trigger fell, a cartridge exploded with a roar, and a big slug plowed up through the back of Lustrell's skull, smashing it. His body was lifeless before it went to the ground.

Standing above it, addressing it quietly, Willet said, "I wish I was back on the Chugwater, where people left people alone."

He picked up the extinguished candle, scraped off a little of the charred wick with his thumbnail to make a brighter light and relit it.

He picked up the fallen .45, and slid it into his holster. He retrieved his ten dollars, and pocketed it. Then he headed toward the stable. He had heard three horses and that was one too many.

He entered the building cautiously. Inside, it was like a dusty wooden cave, tumbledown, hung with cobwebs. The stalls and mangers were half demolished, used by somebody a long time ago for firewood, probably. No harness of any sort hung from the pegs around the walls. The acid odor of old chaff and dung remained, though, and would remain. He took out Lustrell's .45, held his candle aloft, and studied the two horses tied to a half fallen rafter at the far end of the room. All about him, beyond the reaches of the candleshine, were impenetrable black shadows.

The horses, one a nice-looking black thoroughbred, well-groomed, the other a shaggy but powerful roan, were equipped, saddle-gear and all, for about a day's ride, scarcely much longer. The black looked rested. The roan looked as though it had been hurried. Willet wondered if they had come from the village he'd left a few hours ago, where he had met the man in doeskin, and decided no. These were not village horses; these were range horses. Each had emergency canteens, and a rifle in a boot. He concentrated on the black horse. It wasn't a pampered showhorse, as he had at first thought. It was a good, jerky-tough service horse. He came to the conclusion that the black

9

horse could have started off first, and that the roan could have been pushed trying to overtake or pass it.

If that was true, one of the riders could be right here, right now, maybe even watching. One rider was unaccounted for.

Willet called, "If you don't start nothing, I won't."

There was no reply.

Moving warily, he began to look around.

He found the second rider in one of the stalls, supine on the crusty earth. One arm was above his head. There were heel gouges in the ground by his boots. He had been dragged in, and left. His eyes were closed, his twill coat was rumpled and open, and there was a big wet blotch of blood below his upper shoulder. He'd probably been shot outside, Willet decided. He was a heavyset squarish man, with a blocky head, and a clipped black squarish moustache. He opened his eyes, looked at Willet unseeingly, and closed them again. Willet went to the horses, got a canteen, and returned. He set the candle in its own grease on a plank, got to his knees, and examined the man's wound. It was bad enough: it must have really hammered him when the slug hit, but, all in all, there was a chance.

The blood flow had almost stopped, in a jellylike coagulation, but Willet hastened the clotting by applying a handful of cobwebs, one of his grandfather's favorite old remedies. His grandfather also used horse dung, but Willet passed that one up. Once more the man raised his eyelids; he tried to sit up, but Willet stopped him, gently.

"I don't know you," said the man.

"That's right, you don't," said Willet. "What kind of a country you folks run up here anyways? First, who are you?"

"I'm Thomas Lustrell. I own most of the country north of here."

Willet just stared at him.

Finally, he said, "Can you prove it?"

"Of course I can prove it," said the man. In his outrage and indignation, a fleck of bloody foam gathered at the corner of his lip.

Willet believed him. "Then who was the other one, outside?"

"I don't know," said Lustrell. "Some two-bit gunman. I never seen or heard of him before he throwed down on me and let me have it. I was waiting for you, Mr. Shaw."

"I ain't Mr. Shaw," said Willet. "I was offered ten dollars to bring you a message by a man in doeskin in the village some miles back. This-here's the message: Shaw can't make it; he got himself killed in a whorehouse in Fargo, lucky fellow."

"Then I don't know what I'll do," said Lustrell, resting his eyes and reopening them. "Get your money yet?"

"Yes, sir, I got it."

"There's another twenty in it if you take me home," said Lustrell. "It's less than a day from here."

11

"Can you saddle-sit?" asked Willet. Lustrell nodded. "Then why not?" said Willet. "Somebody has to."

"You're being right kind to me," said Lustrell. "And I appreciate it. But if it's all right with you, I'd feel easier if I knew a little more about you."

"I'm Brady Willet."

"And who is Brady Willet?"

"An underfed, out-of-work meandering cowhand, late of *S Reversed,* down in Wyoming on the Chugwater. Praying for heaven, spring, and the next hiring season. What did you want with this Shaw?"

"I wanted to employ him. I thought maybe he could get me out of a little difficulty."

"That was his line of work?"

"Yes. That was his line of work."

"What's the name of this place of yours?"

"The *Box L,*" said Lustrell.

II

For the next ten minutes, Willet was busy. He went out into the stationyard, where his little mare stood docilely groundreined, unquestioning, and got his sole spare shirt, reasonably clean gingham, from his saddlebag, returned and put a not-too-bad pad on Lustrell's wound. He bathed Lustrell's temples from the canteen and gave him a drink, a safe, frugal mouth-wetting drink only. He said to Lustrell, "Is the black horse yours?" When Lustrell nodded, Willet went to the far end of the stable, led the scruffy roan outside, took off her bridle and hung it on her saddlehorn, so her mouth would be free and she could graze and take care of herself, and slapped her lightly. She went off into the night. Back inside, he brought the black thoroughbred into the stall, got Lustrell astride, led them into the yard. Lustrell managed okay. "We better get out of here, and quick," said Willet. "There might be more of same heading this way."

"There might at that," said Lustrell. "We'll take to the brush; follow me. What happened to that man who bushwhacked me?"

"He was taken dead," said Willet. "I'll tell you about it. Later."

"He was fixing to get rid of you," said Mr. Lustrell. "Then rush in and finish me off."

"Very busy," said Willet.

They were passing through a tangle of briars and wildgrape. "You could take the mule road to where it crosses the railroad, and turn, and follow the tracks," said Mr. Lustrell. "But we'll go this way."

"How did I ever get into this for a measly ten dollars?" said Willet.

"Watch them brambles," said Mr. Lustrell.

Hours went by. The going was sometimes good, sometimes rough. With the approach of daylight, Mr. Lustrell, in the lead, became gradually visible. He seemed to be taking the trip well; he was a man of iron, Willet thought. There was the gray of dawn, then sunrise flared, dazzling, in a pink-gold cloudless sky.

"I do believe it's going to be a hot day," said Willet. "And I cherish hot days."

"Hot days in autumn, like hot days in early spring, used to be Indian raiding days," said Mr. Lustrell. "We like 'em now, but they was a time when they was dreaded. I want to know what happened betwixt you and that man back at Dakins Station. You killed him, didn't you?"

"I wouldn't ask you a question like that," said Willet, and dropped once more to the rear.

They were in highlands, around them scoria mainly, slaggy lava, rose-tan in the sun, with here and there small evergreens, wind-twisted and stunted, blackish, about the size and shape of whiskey barrels. The lava seemed endless, in rolling waves and humps, speckled with little weathered pea-sized holes, as though it had been blasted by a giant celestial shotgun. Not far to the north, they could see the mountains, the Little Belts, sheer and bleak and stark, in needle peaks and broad escarpments.

A little after noon, Lustrell, who was about thirty yards ahead, pulled up and waited.

Willet joined him.

They were on a rounded crest. Before them, they could see down into a valley, down on the rooftops of a town in a notch of the uplands: brick chimney mouths, shingles, and a sort of diagram of dusty streets and alleys. Railroad tracks came into the town from the south, terminating just within its limits. There was a roundhouse, repair barns, and a switchyard. There were no tracks north of the town. It would be a spur of the Great Northern, likely, Willet decided. Ending right here. End-of-the-line towns could be mighty mean.

"Here's your money," said Lustrell. He handed Willet twenty dollars.

Willet took it.

He met the eyes of the man beside him, and waited.

"We made it," said Lustrell. "And they're going to be sorry."

Willet asked, "What do you mean, we made it?"

"I'm home."

"Don't tell me that's *Box L*," said Willet.

"That's Winslow, our county seat," said Lustrell. "*Box L*, my home ranch, is west of here. I have other spreads, too. I supervise 'em all from here in town."

"Why?" asked Willet.

"Well, for one thing, I have a growing daughter, Lee. I want to give her advantages. I want her to grow up among people, not cows."

"There's nothing like a railroad town for a growing girl," said Willet.

Missing the irony, Lustrell said, "Maybe I shouldn't have said growing. Maybe I should have said growed. She's nineteen."

"You should have said growed," said Willet.

"Goodbye," said Lustrell. "And thanks again."

"I don't say goodbye until I get you delivered and signed for."

"Whatever you say," said Lustrell. "Lee will be glad to make your acquaintance."

"I doubt if I can even stay to take off my hat. I'm in a hurry. I'm on my way to Canada."

Their surfooted mounts picked their way down the steep slope and they came into the town obliquely, from the southwest, into an outer fringe area, into what looked to Willet like a sparse scattering of substantial homes. The sky had turned leaden, and a light rain was falling. They went down an alley—carriage ruts, grass in the center, grass and board fences at either side—and pulled up at a gate by a barn. Willet dismounted and helped Lustrell down from his saddle. All told, the man was in pretty good shape, but weak. "Tie up," Lustrell said. "The horses can be taken care of later. Get me inside."·

Half-supporting his companion, Willet hitched.

"I don't want you to go to Canada; that can wait," said Lustrell. "I want you to stay with me. I'm desperate. I'll pay you Shaw's wages."

"But I ain't Shaw," said Willet. "I'm just an underfed—"

"Meandering cowhand," said Lustrell. "I know. You've already told me. But back at Aspen Creek, Morgenson picked you. Morgenson knows my problem. His judgment is good enough for me."

"Who is Morgenson, and what is Aspen Creek?"

"Aspen Creek is the village down below Dakins Station. And Morgenson is the man you spoke of dressed in a doeskin shirt."

"He picked me to deliver a message, and that's what I done. He didn't pick me to throw no guns, and that seems to be what you have in mind."

"But you haven't even heard my story."

"And I ain't going to hear it. You can bet on

17

that. I'm getting you inside, and hightailing. I hate this country. It's an abomination to the human race."

"I don't want to lose you. I have a feeling you're a winner."

"Well, I'm not," said Willet. "I've worked back-breaking all my life and got thirty dollars, thirty-five cents, and five stale cinnamon buns."

"But you killed Charlie Derrick, back at the station."

"Was that his name? Who was he?"

"Gunman who used to hang out at the Great Northern Hotel here. I've always heard he was a little better than medium-good."

"Yow!" said Willet. "I'm sure glad I didn't know that at the time. Can you make it inside?"

"Easy," said Lustrell. "You won't reconsider?"

"Not a chance," said Willet. "I'm a fellow that loves his bliss and solitude."

He opened the gate, helped Lustrell up the back walk, and knocked on the back door.

A girl opened to them, and she was about the prettiest thing Willet had ever rested his tired young eyes on. She was dressed in a flare of yellow, had black eyes, long black lashes, and wore her coal black hair in a broad braid down over her left shoulder. He was acutely aware of how he must look to her; shabby, soggy, travel-worn, bleary from a day and a night without sleep. When she saw Lustrell, her face broke into alarm. Lustrell said, "Lee, this is Brady

18

Willet. Charlie Derrick shot me at the station and Mr. Willet, who comes from Shaw—"

"I don't come from Shaw," said Willet. "I come from Wyoming and the *S Reversed*."

"Killed him and brought me home," said Lustrell. "I'm not hurt bad. Run up the street and get Dr. Reynolds."

"Is that the way you get a doctor here?" said Willet. "You just run up a street? You people must do a big business in doctors."

"Take him through the kitchen and up the hall," said the girl. "That'll put you in the parlor, Mr. Willet. There's a sofa there. Make him comfortable. I'll be right back."

In a whiff of sachet, she was gone from them, out into the rain.

Willet assisted Lustrell through the neat kitchen, down a short hall, into a feminine parlor.

There were tied-back lavender draperies at the starched curtains of the two tall windows, and around their tops was a glass-bead fringe. There was flowered carpeting on the floor, and in the center of the room was a round mahogany veneer table with a plaster bowl of crepe paper roses in its center. The air was heavy with the smell of potpourri, spiced flower petals. Willet eased his patient down onto a big black walnut horsehair sofa.

"I can't abide this room," said Lustrell. "I wish I was in my bedroom."

"I wish I was in the Lucky Dollar Poolroom in Yuma," said Willet. "The smell was *cerveza*, chili, and sweat."

They ran out of talk.

When the girl came back, she had behind her a stoutish man all fuss and feathers. He wore bluish-lensed spectacles, and panted a little from the exertion of running. When he examined Lustrell's wound, he said, "Why, you're not bad hurt, Tom. It went clean through your withers muscle, but missed the bone. I'll write out a note for Lee to take to Elvin down to the drugstore. They ain't nothing really wrong with you that willpower plus a few extras won't cure. Fact is, I sure wish I could swap places with you."

He wrote rapidly on a piece of paper. Willet looked over his shoulder: Gum benzoin in powder, balsam of tolu in powder, gum storax, frankincense, myrrh, aloes, (these were in ounces) alcohol 1 gal. To be applied externally for wounds, taken internally for pain.

"Why, that's horse medicine," said Willet. "For horse wounds!"

"We're all God's creatures," said Dr. Reynolds. "It's highly reliable. I always use it myself."

And hundreds of ranchers used it too, and swore by it, Willet knew. He shut up. A wound was a wound.

As the doctor left the room, he said, "Young man, would you step along with me into the kitchen for a minute?"

Willet followed him into the kitchen.

Lowering his voice, the doctor said, "Miss

Lee was talking to me. She knows who you are, and yet she trusts you."

"Knows who I am, and yet she trusts me."

"Yes. And she needs you around. Not for your gun alone, but for you general support. I hope you're aiming to stay a spell."

"I'm skinning out of this country as quick as I can."

"Why?"

"I don't like its ways and means."

The doctor turned his back and walked away, walked out the back door.

And now Miss Lee herself was standing beside Willet.

She said, "Did he give you my message?"

"He gave it," said Willet.

"And what's your answer?"

"My answer is goodbye."

She stood and looked at him a moment, getting organized, he knew, getting ready to let go with her heavy artillery.

She said, "We're in trouble."

He waited courteously, silently.

She said, "Don't stand there and try to look stupid. You don't fool me a bit. Inside, you must be a wonderful person. You found my father there, wounded, a stranger to you. Yet you made a long trip out of you way and brought him home. I believe you now. I don't believe you are from Shaw. You couldn't be. You aren't that kind of man, the Shaw kind. You brought my father home out of compassion, out of a rare kind of humanity."

"I brought him home because he offered me twenty dollars."

"You must have more to you than that!"

"No, ma'am, I don't," he said guilelessly. "It's always been the curse of my life. I'm money-crazy."

Controlling her fury, she went back into the parlor.

He left by the back door, and went down the back walk. The rain had increased, and he could feel its impact against his thin wet clothes. The kitchen garden along the walk was tangled with dead bean vines and the air was gray. The thirty dollars would buy him not only decent food for a while, trail food, but a cheap heavy mackinaw for the Canadian snows.

He opened the board gate, stepped out into the alley, and a man put the muzzle of a .45 between his shoulders. A second unbuckled his gunbelt.

One wore a patched poncho of black gum-rubber, the other a sleazy oilskin slicker. They had the depraved vacant faces of livery stable loafers or barflies. They'd kill a man as quick as they'd kill an ant or chicken. Not only without compunction, but almost without consciousness or thought. Their horses were about ten feet away. "Mount and come with us," said the man in the slicker. Willet unhitched and mounted; Lustrell's horse watched. They rode away, the three of them, down the alley, into the face of the rain.

They left the town, and traveled about eight miles southwest. When they came to a small hollow with a slash of brush and trees, they dismounted and tied Willet to a rotting barkless oak, his hands high above him. Then they waited, smoking cigarettes. About twenty minutes later, another rider came up. Willet crooked his head from the tree bole. The newcomer was one of their kind, one of them. The man in the slicker said, "Did you find them? Did you find the traces?"

"I sure did," said the new arrival. He jingled something, making a metallic clinking in the rain, to prove it.

And Willet knew what he was in for.

By traces, they didn't mean sign or tracks. They meant trace chains, those tugs on a wagon harness extending from the breastband to the whippletree. In a certain kind of viciousness, among night riders and barnburners and their kind, trace chains were for flogging. It was an old and terrible, handed down idea. They didn't kill a man but they did worse. They broke him and taught him a lesson.

The man in the slicker said, "When this is over, go to Nevada or California, or someplace. You hear me?"

Willet said nothing.

While they lashed him, he kept his face pressed hard to the tree. With great control, he kept himself from turning his head again and looking at them, lest a snapping chain-end pull out an eye. Unconsciousness, when it came, was a blessing.

Cold little buckshot rain on his face brought him slowly to groggy consciousness. He had been cut loose, and was on the ground in the mud at the base of the tree. Alone. It was dark. He had no idea of the hour. He got to his knees, to his feet, and made his way to his horse tied to a sapling nearby. His gunbelt was hanging from his saddlehorn, holster and gun. After two failures, he managed to mount.

He retraced his way to Winslow, into its outskirts, down the alley. Lustrell's horse had been stabled. By Miss Lee, probably.

He slid off, hitched, got the gate open, and went up the walk. He knocked on the door with his boot toe.

After a bit, a lamp was lit in the kitchen and the door opened.

Miss Lee, in a plum colored robe, stood before him. Behind her, a clock on the kitchen wall said ten minutes after twelve.

Horrified, she said, "Your dripping blood. What happened?"

"I was waited on," he said. "Can I come in?"

She stepped back for him to enter. As he passed her, he said, "I've changed my mind."

III

She tried to put him in the guest room, with its big brass bed, bolsters and tasseled coverlet, and more artificial flowers, velvet pansies this time, in a cutglass tumbler on the marble top of the washstand. But he said no in a way she knew he meant it. He settled for a little room on the hall to the kitchen instead. It wasn't much, she kept repeating, just a cot, bare floor, and plaster walls, but it was luxury compared to the bunkhouses he'd grown up in, and, besides, though he was careful not to mention it, it had a window to the sideyard, where he could get the hell out any time he wanted to. She brought in a tea kettle of hot water, an enamel basin, a bar of castile soap, and a pile of soft cloths. Though he put up an argument about it, he stripped to the waist and she bathed his back and bandaged it.

Once, she said hoarsely, "It looks like chains," and he said, "Is that so? I didn't notice." She brought him a cup of warm milk and salt and butter—and laudanum. She told him warm milk would make him sleep, and he drank it and slept.

He was slumbering on his cot next morning, in his cheap long underwear busted out at elbows and knees, covered by the blue-gray army blanket pulled up to his chin, when he heard the door open and came up to a sitting position as swiftly as though it had been a Chiricahua raid. It was Miss Lee and Mr. Lustrell. They were beaming solicitously. Miss Lee carried a tray with dishes and things on it. When he saw it, he was appalled.

He said, "What's that?"

"Your breakfast," said Miss Lee.

He wondered if they aimed to feed him, maybe even by force.

He said, "Thank you kindly, but just take it right out. I'll put on my boots and pants and shirt and eat like a human being with you all in the kitchen." They withdrew.

As quickly as he could, he joined them.

They were sitting at the kitchen table, waiting for him, and on the floor by the third chair —the empty one, his—were his saddle bags.

Lee said, "I stabled and fed you mare last night, and watered her and rubbed her down. Just after I'd stabled you. Like I said I would."

"I don't know much what you said last night," said Willet. "I don't know much what I said either. Thank you."

On a platter in the center of the table was a mound of golden scrambled eggs, flecked with something that looked like cracklings in them, a platter of ham slices, the pieces overlapping like when you spread a deck of cards, butter, biscuits, hashbrowned potatoes, four different kinds of fruit preserves and jelly, and a tureen of red gravy from the ham.

Lee served him. Bountifully. Silently, he ate.

When they had finished, Lustrell, leaning against his chairback, said, "My daughter says they flogged you. You wouldn't care to give us the details?"

"No, I wouldn't," said Willet. "The matter will be took care of." His voice was perfectly casual.

After a moment of no conversation, Lee said, "Mr. Willet, you scare me."

Abashed, Willet said, "I'm sorry, Miss Lee. What did I do? Eat too many slices of ham?"

Lustrell gazed at him with affection. He said, "It's almost worth getting shot through the shoulder just to listen to you, son."

Willet picked up his saddlebags, went into his room, and washed and shaved. A new hickory shirt was laid out on the pillow. He got out of the ripped blood-stiff one he wore and put it on.

He then returned to the kitchen. They were still there, still at the table. Again, he joined them on his chair.

He said, "I don't have no idea how long I'm

going to be around this Winslow, and if it's all right with you, I'd like to live here, and use that room I slept in last night."

"That's good news," said Lee.

"So I thought we'd better come to terms," said Willet. "On how much."

"You're our guest," said Lustrell. "They ain't no terms."

"Then I'll put up somewheres else," said Willet. "I don't sponge, and I don't cause hardship."

"What in the hell are you talking about?" said Lustrell, annoyed.

"That man in the doeskin shirt—Mr. Morgenson, you said his name was—back at that little village—Aspen Creek, you said they called it—told me you were poor."

"In a sense, we are," said Lustrell.

"You say you want me to stay here," said Willet stiffly. "But I don't take no unfair advantage of nobody." Slowly, he added, "I been poor myself. It ain't no picnic."

The girl's eyes sparkled moistly. She said, "You know, Daddy, I agree with you. I believe I'd take a shot through the shoulder myself to listen to him."

"Son," Lustrell said gently, "I own most of the rangeland in the county. Didn't Morgenson tell you that, too?"

Willet made no answer.

"There are different kinds of poor," Lustrell explained. "I'm poor in cows. We got plenty of food, plenty of clothes, a good shelter. We're okay along that line."

"Don't let him fool you," said Lee. "He's balanced on the brim of bankruptcy. He walks a razor's edge."

"In what way?" asked Willet.

"He's overextended," said the girl.

"Not quite," said Lustrell.

"Close enough," said Lee. "He has the land, but can't stock it right."

"A common ailment," said Willet. "And a bad one." To Lustrell he said, "Why don't you sell a good chunk of land and buy a good chunk of stock?"

"I couldn't do that," said Lustrell.

"He couldn't do that because it's sensible," said Lee. "It's his lifeblood to be able to say, 'I own most of the county.' "

Willet said, "Then how about this: Why don't you get in touch with some Arizona cattle king, say, and deal for a sizable batch from him, and raise 'em here on halves. Or even thirds? Folks do that. I've heard it said that yearling stock from the south, grazed on northern grass, will pass their southern brothers a couple of hundred pounds. It's a good proposition, and it shouldn't be hard to find a taker."

"Boiled down, I'd be working for him," said Lustrell. "And I couldn't abide that. I ain't made that way."

"You like it best as it is," said Willet.

"Our day'll come," said Lustrell. "Our day'll come."

Lee sighed.

"Why did that gunman Derrick try to kill you the other night back at Dakins Station?" asked Willet.

"We can never prove it, but he was doing a job for Murray Parrish. They knew I was going to bring in Shaw."

"Who is Murray Parrish?" asked Willet.

Lee said, "A newcomer in town. From the Columbia Plateau country in Oregon, they say. Only been around a couple of years. Came in broke, and built himself up, step by step. First, the Judith River Café, then warehouses and business buildings down by the railroad. Then the Great Northern Hotel. By now a mess of other properties, including two spreads out in the foothills."

"How did he do it?" asked Willet.

"By gun and brains," Lustrell said.

"That's a bad combination, and one I ain't troubled with," said Willet. "Why is he after you?"

"He knows our situation," Lustrell said. "He thinks we're a juicy plum. He's tried unsuccessfully to bargain with us. He's trying to break into my holdings."

"But why kill you? asked Willet.

Lustrell said heavily, "Maybe he thinks Lee would be easier to handle than me."

"What kind of appearing man is he?" asked Willet.

"He's about thirty-eight," she said. "And scorns to dress like a townsman. Generally, he's in corduroy or twill or duck, and favors trapper's calf-length boots, his pants stuffed into them. He's got a longish face, muscled and weathered, and killer eyes. I bet he's got a history, before he came here."

"I bet he has, too," said Willet. He got to his feet. "See you later. I think I'll stretch my legs a little."

"Where are you going?" asked Lee.

"Where would you advise?"

"One place I'd stay away from," said Lee, "is the Great Northern Hotel."

It took Willet about eighteen minutes to locate and get to the Great Northern Hotel.

It was in the railroad neighborhood, not far from the roundhouse, and facing the switchyard. There was no rain, but the sky was sooty and blowing, and the cluttered empties were motionless and gray. The building before him, with its sign GREAT NORTHERN R.R. HOTEL, would be privately owned and run, he knew, not company owned. It was of clapboard, with green blistered paint, and at each front corner was a rusty downspout and a rain barrel. On each side of it, up and down the street, were shops with jumbles of merchandise on sidewalk display.

He hitched his gunbelt so that his holster was just a little more comfortable along his thigh, and entered.

The room he found himself in, the lobby, had coarse gray plaster walls, unpainted and unpapered, just as the plasterers's trowels had left them. The carpeting on the floor, thin worn, ruby red, was laid in strips. The furniture was scant, a few chairs, a couple of broken-down settees, and several tall urnlike cuspidors. The desk, which was an old saloon bar, its veneer peeling, was just inside the door, to Willet's left. The clerk behind the desk wore a green celluloid eyeshade and had his sleeves hiked up and tied with butcher's twine. His eyes were furtive, predatory, and his chin and upper throat were a mass of crusty sores. Willet veered over to him and said, "Is Charlie Derrick anywheres about?"

Lustrell had told him that Derrick, the man he'd killed at the station, hung out here.

The clerk said insultingly, "I disremember names."

He turned his back on Willet, and began to fiddle with papers.

Willet said very softly, "You face me when I talk to you. Or you're in trouble."

The clerk wheeled. His manner was stiffly respectful.

"Wait here, please," he said. "I'll ask." He had a squeaky voice.

He came out from behind the desk, went across the lobby and through a door, returned and said, "They's a gentleman over yonder says he might have your information." He pointed.

Willet nodded, and crossed the lobby.

This room was maybe twelve feet square, windowless, and bare-floored. There was a big round table in its center, and a lamp burned on the tabletop because of the lack of windowlight. It was a hideout card room for informal games, Willet decided. He closed the door behind him. A man sat at the table. He had a long, seamed face, little jellylike black eyes, and was dressed in whipcord, his pants stuffed into calf-high boots, the kind of boots that laced up the front. He had a black crooked cigar clamped in his jaw, a deck of cards in his hand, and was amusing himself with one-handed cuts. He said, "Good morning, Mr. Willet."

Willet said, "Good morning, Mr. Parrish."

Drooping the corner of his lip slightly, Parrish said, "I see you've been posted."

"Yes, sir," said Willet.

"You're much younger than I imagined," said Parrish.

"Yes, sir," said Willet.

"They say you've been asking for Charlie Derrick. Still interested?"

"No, sir."

"He's dead. Someone killed him. Maybe Tom Lustrell. It was me you were really looking for, wasn't it?"

"That's right," said Willet.

"Why?"

Willet said nothing.

"I asked you why," said Parrish coldly.

"Maybe I just wanted to look at you," said Willet.

He left the room, and the hotel, and went out onto the street.

IV

This section of Winslow, the railroad section, was a dingy one—as it was in any town, Willet had found: lumber lots, seedy shops and offices, warehouses, bucket-of-blood saloons, corrals. About a block and a half from the hotel, he came to a high board fence with double doors set in it, a wagongate. The doors were closed and on the fence beside them was painted: J. R. Meacham, hide-buyer. Willet opened the doors and stepped inside. Even the smoke and drift from the nearby shunting engines couldn't muffle the terrific stink; it hit him like a hammer, and twisted his stomach.

He was in a small barren yard. Hides were everywhere, some in the open, stacked like poker chips, some under shelters in long sideless sheds. Not far away was a little scrap lumber office roofed in tar paper. He made his way to it, knocked, and, at a yelled invitation, entered.

There was a cannonball stove, a few broken-down chairs, and a battered desk; above the desk was a cheap lithograph of an open-air prizefight. There were hides here, too, a stack of them in the corner, and a man stood by them examining the topmost. He was a chubby man, grimy, in blood and grease smeared denims, and his face, when he turned it to Willet, was mild and shrewd and fatherly. Hide-buyers were like horse traders, or jewelers, for that matter; they thrived or went broke on the grounds of what they knew about their trade.

Willet said, "You Mr. Meacham, as per the sign outside?"

"Am," said Mr. Meacham. "Got some hides to sell?"

"No," said Willet.

"Ever aim to sell any?"

"Don't know at this date."

"Wisely spoke," said Mr. Meacham. "Come here."

Willet stood beside him.

Meacham pointed to the hide on the top of the pile. "What do you see there?"

"I see a dry stiff hide."

"That would be the common answer. Would you care to know what a dealer sees?"

Willet nodded.

"He sees it accurate, and at a glance. Because he knows just what he's looking at. With his eye, he draws a line from the center of the top of the hide to the center of the bottom.

35

On each side of this line, in the middle, he gauges a wide strip, which must have quality and perfection. These two sections, one on each side, make up 'the bends.' The little strip crosswise above them, to each outer edge, is called 'the range.' He also looks at this, and judges it. The far outside edges, down along the sides, are called 'the belly offal.' The little ragged part at the top, the part where the head was, is called 'the cheeks and faces.' Know that, and one quick look and you see everything, its quality, how perfect it is, everything. You just need to whip your eyes across it—bends good, range okay, belly offal okay, cheeks okay."

"Forevermore," said Willet, impressed.

"It should weigh twenty-five pounds or better when raw, twelve pounds or better dried, fifteen pounds or better dried and salted. If it comes from a small or young animal, a sheep, a goat, a calf, or so forth, it's called a kip. What brings you here?"

"A hide-buyer gets around," said Willet. "And people get in to see him. He must get to know his country and people pretty well."

"Tolerable, tolerable."

"I come to beg for a little information."

"Passing out information is one of my favorite enjoyments. Let's sit down."

They took chairs.

"You know Mr. Tom Lustrell?" asked Willet.

"Since we were whippersnappers."

"What do you think of him?"

"He'll do."

This, Willet knew, was the highest praise one man could give another. Just as "He won't do" was the worst condemnation.

"He'll do with me, too," said Willet.

They sat gravely inspecting each other.

"He's like a man in a sulky on a oval racetrack," said Mr. Meacham unhappily. "He's going mighty fast, but he ain't going nowhere. I sure wish he'd drive back to the barn and unharness."

"He says his day'll come," said Willet defensively.

"Let's hope it ain't his day of doom," said Mr. Meacham.

"You referring to Mr. Murray Parrish?"

"I never refer to Murray Parrish. I'm speaking of things in general."

"Like what?"

"He's got a mule-streak in his brain that keeps whispering land is everything. If he don't meet his demise from a .45, he'll get it worse, from the sheriff's hammer."

"Who would demise him with a .45?"

"You're making me uneasy. The party of the second part you just mentioned."

"Parrish?"

"You spoke it; I didn't."

"Why?"

"Parrish wants to buy the *Box L*. For cigarette papers and matches. Tom Lustrell won't sell. Wouldn't sell for anything. It's his childhood home."

Willet asked, "Why does Parrish want it?"

"Because it adjoins one of his, Parrish's

worthless little rocky-scrabbled spreads, the miserable *Double Star*. He wants to expand, he says. Expanding the *Double Star* by adding the *Box L* is like expanding a useless old moose tail by adding a moose."

"How far west is it?" asked Willet.

Lustrell had said the *Box L* was west of Winslow.

"Scarcely a few hours' ride. Why?"

"I thought I might go out and look it over."

"They don't take kindly to strangers."

Willet asked, "Why?"

"How should I know? I guess it's just in their nature. Some folks is different from other folks. I'm just the opposite. I take kindly to strangers."

"Ha-ha. All the time with your hand in your pocket keeping it on your Barlow knife, I bet."

"Is that any way to talk to a man old enough to be your father? And, besides, I've had some bitter experiences. And I don't have no Barlow knife. I have a pocket pistol. Furthermore, I ain't done so with you."

"Are you saying you trust me?"

"Let's don't rush things. I sure as hell wish I knowed a little more about you. But don't bother to tell me. I have a feeling I'll learn."

"Before I leave," said Willet, "I'd like to ask you one more question. Where can I find these men?" He described the three men who had whipped him, the man in the slicker, the man in the poncho, and the man who had arrived with the trace chains. He described them in great detail, the bridges of their noses, the color of their eyes, their heights and weights, their approximate ages. This was his first going-over. Then he went into pimples, gap teeth, calluses, odds and ends of tiny facial and hand scars.

Meacham listened fascinated. "You don't miss much."

"Plenty," said Willet. "A good apache on a war party can tell from horse-sign males from females, by how they let down their droppings and make their water on the mesquite. I never could get the hang of that."

"What you want with these men?"

"They chain-flogged me."

At first, deeply moved, Meacham seemed not to hear. Then he asked carelessly, "Why."

"They wanted me to go to Nevada or California, or someplace."

"I hate to keep at it, by *Why?*"

"They thought I was a gunman Mr. Lustrell had brought home with him."

"Are you?"

"No, indeed. As a matter of fact, Mr. Lustrell didn't bring me home. I brought him home."

"Don't talk fancy on me. Are you a gunman?"

"No, sir."

"You don't mean, 'yes, sir'? You look like a little sack of mighty mean rattlesnakes to me."

"I can't help being little," said Willet. "And I ain't mean."

"Say something in your favor," said Meacham.

Willet studied, trying to think of something in his favor.

39

"Go ahead," said Meacham. "I'm waiting."

"I never break my word," said Willet at last. "It's like pulling hens' teeth getting it out of me, but once I give it, I never break it. Will that do?"

Meacham's face broke into a monstrous grin. He thrust out his palm. "That'll do," he said. "Shake my hand."

Willet shook it, got up, and left. His face burned with embarrassment. What had got into the man?

The only time Willet ever shook hands was hiring on with a new boss.

He and his friends rarely shook hands, even on being introduced to someone. They just nodded. A nod was a heap better than a handshake on being introduced. If you didn't like the person, you could give him the faintest of nods and a poker face; if you liked him, you could give him a big nod and a smile.

He got his mare from the Lustrell stable without disturbing anyone. The back porch and the back of the house looked dank and gave off a feeling of emptiness. Inside, Willet decided, they weren't doing much stirring, just a slew of worrying.

He rode down the alley, turned into another, and a little later the town was behind him.

He bore due west.

The grass was good, and got better. Cows were scarce, though, hardly existent at all. About midafternoon, he did, however, pass through a pitiful little gathering of them. They carried the *Box L* brand, and told him he was in

40

Lustrell country. The sky was low and gray, like rolls of soggy wool, and, while there was no rain, things were dismal. To the north and west were the Little Belts, vague slate crags in the humidity, and somwhere at their base, in their foothills, he had been told, lay Parrish's *Double Star*.

It was about five o'clock, and the high plain was already darkening into murky night, when he guided his mare up the rise of a little knoll to its crest, to get his bearings. At the top of the knob, he came into a dark grove.

He drew up, leaned back on his cantle, and considered. The lights of the ranch house and its buildings were just below him, down the slope.

He was about to move forward, down the hill, when he heard the commotion to his left.

The indistinct figure of a horseman rode through the trees and undergrowth toward him, crackling and snapping twigs and branches as he came.

Now the man was alongside him, shoving his face into Willet's.

He said, "Beckett? Bill Beckett? You got my money? What held you up?" His voice was friendly, conspiratorial.

Before Willet could answer, the man said, "You're not Bill Beckett." There was the lump of a gun in his off-rein hand.

" 'Evening," said Willet. "Excuse me if I jumped. I didn't hear you, you come up so quiet."

"Who are you?" the man asked roughly.

41

"That's hard to say," said Willet amiably. "Why do you want to know?"

"I'd advise you to answer," said the man.

"I'm knowed as Arizona," said Willet. "Sometimes Little Arizona, but I don't much care for the 'Little.' Let's make it a swap. Who are *you?*"

"Julian Craycroft," said the man. "I'm foreman here. You got business with me?"

"This *Box L?*" asked Willet.

"It sure as hell is," said Craycroft. "I never seen you before. Where do you call home?"

"The Lucky Dollar Poolroom, down in Yuma," said Willet. "It's a kind of orphanage, you might say."

"This land's posted," said Craycroft. "What trespassers that makes it to the courts are prosecuted. We don't like drifters."

"Oh, drifters are all right," said Willet goodnaturedly. "When you finally get to be one of them. But I ain't a drifter. I came here because I was sent for. A Mr. Tom Lustrell sent for me. This-here is his place, isn't it?"

"He has lots of places. This happens to be one of them. He ain't here. What's he want with you?"

"Where can I find him?" asked Willet.

"Did you say he sent for you?" said Craycroft. "Why?"

"If he isn't here, where would he be?" asked Willet.

"I'm about to have supper," said Craycroft. "Come down and join me."

When Willet pretended to hesitate, Craycroft

pressed him. "I got a good cook."

"If you say so," said Willet. "I come a long way."

They descended the dark hillside, made their way in and out of the cluster of well-kept ranch buildings, to the railed back veranda of a two-storied residence. Here, they got down and tied up. The kitchen windows gleamed softly golden with lamplight.

Inside, they sat at the kitchen table. The room was high-ceilinged, with scrubbed floor of resinous pine. There was a battery of cupboards, varnished lemon yellow, a zinc-lined sink with a pump, and a large kerosene lamp overhead, raised and lowered by little pulleys and a rope fastened to a cleat on the doorjamb. It was the showiest kitchen Willet had ever dreamed of.

He studied his host. Craycroft was a gaunt man, sinew tough, in worn range clothes. His hard little eyes were sunk behind the rosy blade of a sun-peeled nose, and his lips, flaked with dead skin, chewing tobacco stained, and pushed together tight, said that he was a man that could never be wrong. The world could be wrong, but he couldn't.

Willet asked, "You live here?"

"Yes."

"I mean here in this house," said Willet.

"That's right."

"You don't often see a foreman living in the big-house," said Willet.

"This foreman does," said Craycroft. "He ain't only the foreman, he's the manager, too.

43

And somebody has to. Since Mr. Lustrell and daughter has outgrowed us, and gone elsewhere."

That was no way for a foreman to talk of his boss to a stranger, sarcastic, but Willet made no comment.

The bunkhouse cook came in from the outside cookhouse through the back door, his arms loaded with trays and small cast iron buckets and saucepans. Craycroft said, "I hope you brought enough for two."

"I did," said the cook. "I seen the both of you a-coming." He was a compact little man, sloppy in his movements. Busily, he shuttled from cupboards to table, setting out plates, tureens, cups, tableware. He then served the food from the buckets and trays; sometimes he used his fingers, sometimes he used a big iron spoon. When he had finished to his satisfaction, he left.

Willet, always interested in food, looked it over. Halfcooked short ribs, watery mashed turnips with nuggets of boiled potatoes, a bowl of overfried onions, butter and rocky-looking biscuits, stringy dried-peach jam, apple sauce with cinnamon and cloves. It looked about as appetizing as the raw side of a new bearskin. But food was food. Willet and his host began to eat.

Craycroft said with heavy amiability, "Would you mind running through that again? Why was it Mr. Lustrell sent for you?"

"Cowhand, I guess. That's my trade."

"Nobody takes on cowhands at this time of year."

"What else could it be?" said Willet. "That's all I know, tending cows."

"Is that what you done home in your poolroom?"

"They ain't no cows in a poolroom," explained Willet. "So nobody tended none. But they sure as hell was a heap of *talk*, going back and forth, about tending cows."

"I'm going to ask you once more," said Craycroft. "Why did he bring you north?"

"My father done his father a favor once. He was trying to repay."

"Repay how?"

"Trying to keep moths and rust and evil companions from corrupting me."

Craycroft stared at Willet, his eyes burning into him, baffled.

"Can I go now?" asked Willet.

"Ain't you going to thank me for the meal?"

"I'll thank Mr. Lustrell for it."

"You can go," said Craycroft.

As Willet rode away, he passed the rear of the little cedar-log cookhouse. The cook was outside, in a glow of light from his back door, scrubbing his ironware vigorously with lava grit and lye soap. Willet sidled up his mare, brought her to a stop, and said, "I don't know when I ever tasted such nice hot-flavored apple sauce."

"You like it?" said the cook, pleased.

"It almost took the skin off my tongue. I almost suspicioned you put cayenne pepper in it."

"Nobody puts pepper in apple sauce, son."

"Then how did you do it?"

"Just cinnamon and cloves."

"I can hardly believe it. My mouth still feels like it's holding a redhot horseshoe."

"I'll let you in on a little secret," said the cook. "I always fortify the cloves with a little oil-of-clove toothache medicine."

"I knew there had to be a secret about it somewhere," said Willet. "Could you tell me how far it might be to the *Double Star* ranch house?"

"About half a mile. But I wouldn't cross the line from here was I you. We don't mix, and they're mighty nervous people."

"About half a mile?" said Willet. "So close? I thought it was back in the foothills."

"The ranch itself does run back into the foothills," said the cook. "But the buildings are yonder, just over that rise." He lifted his arm and pointed. "The early owners of *Box L* and *Double Star* were kin, they tell me, and built close together."

Willet asked, "You got a man working here called Bill Beckett?"

"No," said the cook. "And that's a name despised on *Box L* land. He runs the *Double Star*, for Murray Parrish."

V

The *Double Star* buildings were, as the cook had said, just over the rise. *Box L,* with its barns and worksheds and windmill, its two wells and three corrals, had almost seemed a village. Now they were blocked from view by the low hill spine and what Willet rode into put him in mid of a desolate back country outpost. The small stable was about twenty feet behind the squat cabin, and the two structures were joined at their corners by a mauled rail fence, making the corral. Off to one side was a second cabin with a lean-to at its rear; this, Willet decided, would be the ranch bunkhouse, cookhouse, too, maybe, and general crew quarters, with the lean-to being a forge and toolshed. The night was chill black, clammy and vaporous. There was no one in sight. Light showed in the ranch house cabin, and in the bunkhouse. Willet got down from his saddle and tied up at one of the corral rails. He knocked at the cabin's puncheon door.

A man came up behind him, swing the door open by shoving over his shoulder, and said, "Let's go in."

They stepped inside. The man closed the door and dropped a bar.

"I'm Bill Beckett," he said. "Who are you, and what do you want?"

He was a little less than medium tall, gawky, hateful-looking. His eyes were just charcoal flecks between greasy folds of skin. His teeth were mossy and rotten-looking. He stood and walked with his knees bent and his elbows out, as though he had just lighted from a jump, or was just getting ready to jump. He was an ugly-looking mortal, and a deadly-looking one.

Willet said, "I just come over from Mr. Craycroft at *Box L.*"

He paused.

There were no fireworks. Beckett waited, not hostilely but expectantly.

Willet said. "He wants me to tell you he was on top of the little hill, but you never showed up with his money."

"You work at *Box L?*" asked Beckett.

"No, sir," said Willet. "I'm just a cowhand bound for Canada that went and got himself sidetracked."

"What particular money did he have reference to, I wonder?" said Beckett.

This was a trap question, feeling Willet out, Willet realized.

He said, "He didn't go into no details. He just give me supper and asked me to carry you the message."

"Would you carry one back?"

"Why not?" said Willet agreeably. "It's on my way."

"Tell him I wasn't there because I was called into town by Mr. Parrish."

"Will he want to know why this Mr. Parrish called you?"

"Tell him Mr. Parrish says Tom Lustrell has brought him a gun artist back to Winslow with him."

"I think I can remember that," said Willet.

"And don't tell nobody else," said Beckett threateningly. "Then get on your way to Canada. Understand?"

"Yes, sir," said Willet.

"Now get out," ordered Beckett. "You saddle bums tote nits and bedbugs, and we got enough already."

Willet left the cabin, unhitched, and headed directly back to town.

Craycroft, through Beckett, was working for Parrish. Everybody seemed to be working for Parrish. The bad feeling between *Box L* and *Double Star* was just a show being put on for the public. Put on as far as Craycroft and Parrish were concerned anyhow.

Willet wondered what he had gotten into.

There was no need to mention it to the Lustrells.

Yet.

* * *

49

It was a little before twelve when he got back to Winslow. He rode immediately to Railroad Row, toward the Great Northern Hotel. He was so mad he decided to have it out with Murray Parrish right now, face to face. Then he thought, *Have what out?*—and knew he'd better cool off a little first. If he disclosed what he'd learned at the *Box L,* and the *Double Star,* and didn't have anything more to go on, it wouldn't help things. It could just make things worse.

The shops along the tracks had taken in their pavement merchandise and were closed for the night. He left his mare at a post before a pawnshop. He walked past an owl restaurant or two, an occasional hole-in-the-wall saloon blaring light and piano music, but mainly the building fronts were dark and soggy. To his left, over in the switchyards, a solitary shunting engine gave off the deep red glow of a coal eye and coughing puffs of cloudy steam.

He was just thinking about the mackinaw he was going to buy, and weighing it against a sheepskin instead, when he felt a touch on his wrist, and saw a tough little boy of about eleven standing beside him, skull-faced and hard-jawed—the kind of youngster that had been alley born and alley raised. The boy said, "Mr. Meacham sent me to watch for you."

"You mean Mr. Meacham, the Hide-buyer?" said Willet.

The boy handed him a small wad of paper, and was gone.

Willet stepped to the window of a watch repair shop showing a nightlight, uncrumpled the paper, and held it to the diamond weave of the heavy wire protective grille. He read:

> *The man you spoke of in the slicker is George Duffy, fry cook at the Judith River Café. The man in the poncho is Lester Meadows and the other one is August Ritter—all is dregs, all is friends. Ritter and Meadows has coffee with Duffy every night around midnight at the café. Can you still remember the names of the parts of a hide?*
>
> *Yrs, J. R. Meacham*

The Judith River Café was about halfway between the Great Northern Hotel and the Meacham hide-yard. Willet had passed it several times. On one side of it was a livery barn, and on the other a vacant lot with a stack of old lumber overgrown with now withered morning glory vines. The café itself was built with planks going up and down and placed close to the sidewalk. It had a couple of secondhand house windows set in its front. Every inch of glass of these windows had been lettered with whitewash printing: *Bean Soup & Gravy 25¢, Railroad Stew Big Bowl 10¢, Chocolate Pie and Coffee 10¢.* Willet turned the big door knob and walked in.

A stained wooden counter with high three-legged stools extended from the doorway to a partition at the back. The walls were dirty, the floor was dirty and littered, and a row of fly-paper streamers lumpy with dead flies hung from the ceiling. It was about as foul an eatery as Willet had ever been in, but he had a feeling that fronting the railroad and all it was a real money-maker.

Two men sat on their stools down by the partition, over mugs of coffee, chatting with a third man behind the counter, a man with a dishcloth stuck in his belt. Willet looked them over as he advanced. One of the men in front of the counter had cheeks covered with thin dirty hair, and blinked through bloodshot eyes; this was the man of the poncho, all right. The man beside him, dressed in the tight-fitting castoffs, was the one who had come up with the chains. The man behind the counter, gaunt-jawed, loselipped, was the man of the slicker, the one who had been their leader. He had a pair of long-handled pliers in his hand, and was tightening a nut on a meat-saw blade.

"Chain-whipped anybody lately?" asked Willet as he came up.

He kept his thumb carelessly in the neighborhood of his gunbutt, gunfighter style. Many a counter had a shotgun under it.

They swiveled their heads toward him, and froze.

Duffy, the fry cook, laid the pliers and the saw slowly on the countertop.

"Whoever you are," said Duffy, "you seem set on some kind of disturbance. Just turn around and leave. I don't know you."

"You're going to know me mighty soon," said Willet.

The thing that bothered them most was that he

seemed to have forgetten he was wearing a gun.

Willet stood silent a long moment, absorbed in thought.

Sneeringly, but not sneeringly enough to set things off, the man named Ritter said, "What you pondering?"

"I had it in my mind," said Willet mildly, "to flog you all, like you done me. But I've decided no."

They all smiled derisively. Duffy said, "One man flogging three. You don't hear of that very often. And where's your chain?"

"I passed a well a piece back," said Willet. "I aimed to use the well-chain."

"And we'd wait here while you went to get it?" said Meadows.

"You'd wait here," said Willet. "Back there behind the partition, out of sight."

"You mean you'd tie us?" asked Duffy.

"Tying wouldn't be necessary," said Willet.

They gaped at him, bewildered.

"You'd be dead," Willet explained.

In a dry sandy voice, Duffy said, "You'd shoot us, and take us behind the partition, and get the chain, and *then* flog us? You'd flog dead men?"

"A flogging is a flogging," said Willet. "And I always pay my debts. But, like I said, I've changed my mind."

"You're a professional gun thrower, ain't you?" said Duffy. "We're all dead men this minute, ain't we?"

"Maybe not," said Willet. "If you do what I

say. Make a tight fist with your right hand. That's right. Now hold your arm out a little, slow. Now turn the underside of your wrist up. What's that little cord that pushes up through the skin down your arm to your thumb?"

"That's the tendon that works my fingers," said Duffy.

"Correct," said Willet. He picked up the pliers from the counter. They were general utility farm pliers. At each side of the pliers' head was a groove, for wire snipping. He took up a nearby fork, and clipped off a tine. They watched him, horrified.

He said, "You didn't try to kill me, so why should I want to kill you? All you did was flog me. So what I'm going to do is fix it so you can't flog nobody else. I'm going to clip your right hand wrist tendons."

He looked at them. They were wild-eyed and broken men.

Ritter asked, "What'll happen to the hand?"

"It'll wither and curl up," said Willet. "And shrink. Maybe to the size of a dressed squab. But you'll still have it."

All vitality gone from his voice, Duffy said, "And there's no way out?"

"Why, yes, there is," said Willet. "You could catch a freight train for Nevada or California or someplace. Who put you on to me?"

"Murray Parrish," said Duffy.

"How much did he pay you?" asked Willet.

"Five dollars apiece," said Duffy.

"I'll take it," said Willet.

"We don't have it no longer," said Ritter. "We spent it that night, later, in celebration."

A couple of bottles of whiskey, a deck of cards, and a barn lantern, under a railroad culvert probably, thought Willet.

"I'm sorry I wasn't there," he said. "I like celebrations."

After a pause, he said, "I'm going now. And don't try to shoot me in the back. Unless you're sure you can do it."

"We're sure we can't," said Duffy. "And we wouldn't anyhow."

The Lustrells were in their kitchen when Willet came in, Lee cutting up and fiddling with a piece of cheesecloth, fashioning it into something or other domestic, Mr. Lustrell at the table, elbows before him on the tabletop, staring blankly ahead of him, shredding some vile-looking twist tobacco onto his palm, and cramming it into a stubby pipe. Willet had a feeling that they had been waiting for him, concerned for his safety. He was touched.

"Here he is," said Miss Lee.

"And hale and hearty," said Willet.

"You remember Aspen Creek?" said Mr. Lustrell.

"The village on yonder side of Dakins Station?" said Willet. "Where I got started on all this?"

"That's the place," said Mr. Lustrell. "Would I be asking too much to ask you to do us a favor? Something's happened. I don't know just what, but I have the feeling the Lustrells are headed for real disaster. I want Lee out of it. You understand?"

"Yes, sir," said Willet.

"Morgenson is the only friend I've got," said Mr. Lustrell. "He's like a blood brother to me. I want you to go to Aspen Creek and tell him I aim to send Lee down to him in a couple of days, and I want him to hide her out somewheres until this is over."

"Why don't I take her with me?" said Willet.

"He'll want a couple of days to scout around and fix things up."

Willet said, "Why don't you go along with her?"

"Because I wasn't created that way."

"I like you," said Willet. "I've taken your money. I'm your man. I'll be staying with you."

They beamed at him.

He asked, "Is there a quicker way of getting there?"

"Yes," said Mr. Lustrell. "There's a short-cut."

There was a sharp but courteous double-tap at the back door. Lee went to it and opened it.

Murray Parrish stepped in and stood in the lamplight, wicked little black eyes, whipcord pants, short trapper's boots, and all, just as Willet had last seen him at the Great Northern Hotel. He tried to stand humble, but couldn't quite make it. He said, "I was just riding

56

around, and seen your light, and something came over me and I knew I had to come in right now and get it over."

"Get what over?" said Mr. Lustrell. "I got no complaint. Things are okay from my viewpoint."

"Have a seat, Mr. Parrish," said the girl.

"I couldn't do that," said Parrish. "Not where I'm not wanted. But thank you, ma'am. I see you still got your house guest."

"If you mean me," said Willet, "they still have."

"Did you have anything special in mind you wanted to discuss?" asked Mr. Lustrell.

"Yes," said Parrish.

"Then let's get to it," said Mr. Lustrell.

Parrish said, "I want to make you a final offer on the *Box L*. We'll let your foreman out there, Craycroft, and my man at the *Double Star*, talk it over and set the right price. Nobody can say that wouldn't be fair enough."

"The *Box L* isn't for sale," said Mr. Lustrell.

"The boys in them two places is fomenting against each other," said Parrish. "It could work into something mighty bad for the whole country. Don't you agree?"

"We'll cross that bridge when we come to it," said Mr. Lustrell.

"When it's already afire?" said Parrish. "You can't cross a burning bridge. It's too late, then."

"If buying my ranch is your remedy," said Lustrell, "I don't like it."

"That's just one of my remedies," said Parrish. "I got another."

"What is that?" asked Lee.

"You buy the *Double Star* from me," said Parrish.

Jarred, Mr. Lustrell said, "What price?"

He wasn't interested, just curious.

Parrish said, "For nothing, really. Buy it at sheepland prices. That's what about half of it should be, anyways, sheepland."

A gleam came into Mr. Lustrell's eyes. "I'll think it over."

The girl said Fiercely, "He won't think it over. The answer is no."

"Under one ownership," said Parrish, "there wouldn't be no trouble atwixt them. Gun-trouble can be a heap sorrowful. I know. I've seen it."

"So have I," said Willet.

"I'm sure you have," said Parrish.

"By the way, Mr. Parrish," said Willet. "I just come from the Judith River Café. You may have to get yourself a new fry cook. He was talking with a couple of his friends, an August Ritter and a Lester Meadows. They was speaking about the three of them catching a freight for California."

Expressionlessly, Parrish asked, "What took you *there?*"

"Meat and rice and gravy, twenty-five cents," said Willet.

Parrish nodded stiffly to Lee, to Mr. Lustrell, and left.

Willet said, "I guess I'd better be getting to

bed. I want to start early, probably before you're up. You say there's a shortcut?"

"Take the stage pike in front of our house here, south," said Mr. Lustrell. "Go about a mile. You'll come to Aspen Creek, to the ford over it. Don't cross the creek but turn off the pike and follow the creek downstream. There's a horse-and-foot path along the stream bank. Maybe in about twelve hours you should end up in the village. Anyone there can tell you where to find Morgenson."

"There'll be a cold breakfast waiting for you in the windowbox," said Lee.

"Put it in a old paper sack, if you've got one," said Willet. "And I'll eat it in the saddle, on the way."

"Do you want me to pack some traveling food, too?" asked the girl.

"Maybe. Because I hope to make time. I want to get back," said Willet. "Put in a can of pork and beans, say. And some of them leftover corndodgers there on the table."

She went with him to his bedroom door. His hand on the knob, he said, "Take care of yourself while I'm gone."

"I will," she said. "And you do the same."

"I'll be all right," he said. "I'll enjoy the airing."

"You make the whole thing sound like a picnic," she said.

"Well, it ain't," he said. "Good night."

He waited in his room, in the dark, cross-legged on the floor, for about forty-five minutes.

Finally, he heard them go to bed. He went to the kitchen, got his packet of food from the widowbox, returned, shut his door, and left the house by the bedroom window. The sky was dazzling clear, with a big white harvest moon, and there was an autumnal fragrance from the fallen apples beneath the tree in the sideyard. Upstairs, lamps went out, one, two. He went down the garden walk to the barn, saddled in the dark, led his mare out into the alley and mounted.

The full moon was silvery and luminous as he rode along the stage pike. He ate his breakfast.

When he reached the creek and the ford, he turned downstream, as he had been instructed, down the creekside path.

. . . .
. . . .
. . . .
. . . .
. . . .
. . . .
. . . .
. . . .
. . . .
. . . .

VI

With daylight, he saw that Aspen Creek was an
all-weather stream, for he passed patches of
marsh and bog, with a kind of reed grass and
cattails and rank jimpson weed. The creek itself
was bordered with underbrush and a con-
tinuous hedge of mottled willows and alders. It
looked sluggish and almost stagnant. Its life
would be ugly, probably, gar and mud turtle
and weasel. He didn't know about Montana,
but in Arizona it would be a good place to get
snake bit, or spider bit, or to pick up leeches.
The night had been chilly, but the day had
turned out scorching. Midmorning, he entered
a thicket of aspens, and a few minutes later
came into a clearing.

It was a small clearing, and in its center was
a sorry little hut painted with tar. The path
passed about three feet from its open front

door. On one side of it, on the near side as
Willet came up, a man and a woman were putting out fresh meat for jerky, hanging inch
wide strips of beef on a rack made of barbed
wire and poles. The women, in her thirties but
toothless, wore patched gingham, and had a
jaw like a burro. The man was about the same
age; his unshaven chin was bristly, and he wore
droopy denim pants and a dirty, flannel shirt
fastened at the collar buttonhole with a piece
of fishline.

They greeted Willet cautiously.

Willet stopped and dismounted. He said,
"Nice-looking meat. It'll go mighty good a little later with a hot bowl of soup, when you're
snowed in."

"It cost me a mountain of cordwood to get
it," said the man. "I worked day-labor for nigh
three weeks to get it. And I got a bill of sale to
prove I own it, in case you're an Association
man."

"Not me!" said Willet. "I'm a hobo. Name
of Brady Willet."

"Mr. and Mrs. Dunningham," said the
woman. They were becoming more friendly.
"Pleased to make your acquaintance, Mr.
Willet. Can I get you a drink of water, say? Or
maybe something a little stronger?"

"I believe not," said Willet, smiling. He
liked them.

"Mighty fine gun you're carrying for a
hobo," said Mr. Dunningham admiringly.

"Is it?" said Willet. "I never noticed. I got it

one night in the dark in a sort of trade with a passing acquaintance."

They sensed this was a delicate subject, and didn't follow it up.

Willet said, "Last house I stopped at, the lady packed up some vittles. Why don't we see what we've got and have us a party?"

"We'd relish that," said Mrs. Dunningham.

Dunningham went into the hut, came out with three homemade willow chairs, and placed them in a little circle. Willet went to his mare and got Lee's paper sack. They seated themselves. Hand to hand, they passed the sack around the circle, looking into it, selecting, eating. It contained fried chicken, a dozen hard-boiled eggs, bread, a big piece of pound cake, and a little tin can with a key to it. Dunningham inspected the can. It said POTTED MEAT. Canned potted meat was new these days, Willet had heard, and was a big fad. Dunningham wound the key and opened the can. The gummy substance it contained startled him. He sniffed it.

"Pee-yoo!" he said, then apologized for his comment. "Excuse me."

When they had finished eating, the can of potted meat was still untouched.

"What are you going to do with it?" asked Dunningham.

"I'm going to leave it here," said Willet. "Can't you use it?"

"I believe I can," said Dunningham, brightening. "I'll use it for bait in my turtle trap."

"Well, I think I'll be moving," said Willet, arising. "Thank you all for your hospitality."

"Where are you headed?" asked Mrs. Dunningham.

"I've never seen Florida yet," said Willet.

"Florida!" said Dunningham, impressed. "You surely cover the miles!"

"That was mighty delicious cake," said Mrs. Dunningham. "I always pay favors with favors. Wait a minute."

She went into the house and came back. She had a horseshoe nail in one hand, and claw hammer in the other. She shoved them toward him.

He made no move to accept them. "They'd be handy to have along," he said. "A hammer and nail and all. But I don't generally carry no extra weight."

"A far-traveling gent like this one don't want to carry no tool chest," said Dunningham, reproving her.

"This-here hammer is my favorite household weapon," she said. "I use it on mice, beetles, and sometimes husbands. I ain't giving it to him. I'm just lending it to him. I'm giving him the nail." They were standing near Willet's mare. Mrs. Dunningham pointed to the ground. "His mare has got a loose nail in her near hind shoe."

The two men stared at the packed earth.

She was right, Willet saw. Wherever there was a near hind hoofprint there was an extra scar in the track, the mark of a loose nail.

He lifted the hoof and examined the shoe. A nail had been pulled out. A little, not too much, but enough to leave sign that a man almost blind could follow. *Pulled* out. You could see the scratched metal on the sides of the nailhead where an implement had grasped it. He had been marked so that we would be easy to follow.

When had it been done? In the Lustrell stable, probably.

While Parrish was inside, likely, with his visit to divert them, his offer to sell them the *Double Star* to hold their attention. They wanted to know all about Brady Willet, where he went, what he did. Skillfully, almost professionally, Willet drew the old nail and replaced it with the new.

He handed Mrs. Dunningham her hammer.

"This might have saved my life," he said.

"Might have, at that," said Dunningham. "A throwed shoe can be bad."

Willet stepped into his stirrup and swung his leg over his saddle. He said, "Should anyone drop by and ask about me, tell them the truth. Tell them I came and went. No need to get yourselves dragged into anything."

The man said, "You on the run?"

Willet shook his head.

Mrs. Dunningham said, "Don't fret about us getting dragged in. Any way we can help?"

"Just tell them the truth," said Willet and rode away.

Until about the middle of the afternoon, the

creekbank path wound through an interlocking belt of willow and aspen, and then, abruptly, he crossed an area of shallow eroded gullies with a million rabbits scampering through dead sage runnels. Beyond this open space, an old burnover, he decided, he entered a cottonwood forest, ancient, silent, the breathless air slanted with moted sunrays. All day he had ridden alertly, with his ears keyed for the sounds of riders behind him, but had heard nothing. He was sure, however, that they were there.

Beyond the cottonwoods, it was open space again, and the path—leaving the creekbank for a while because of the roughness of the terrain —wove among great glazed globular boulders. Where the trail was crazily serpentine, he got down, tied his mare behind a big smooth triangular stone, and sat on his heels to wait. The sun was low. This meant they would be hurrying, getting less careful.

He waited about an hour. Then all at once he heard them, the hoofbeats along the path, in and out of the boulders, coming at a floundering canter.

Willet got up and stepped out into the center of the trail. There were two of them, and they were nearly over him. They reined up like maniacs.

They were so close that at first it seemed all enormous horses' chests and heads and bridles, leather bridle straps and brass buckles, flying streamers of slaver. Then loomed the men be-

behind the horses' ears, half raised in their saddles.

One, red-eyed and hollow-cheeked, his mouth open in a mute shout, was dressed in faded brown duck. The other, squat and muscular, bloated-lipped, in a tossing quill vest and bearskin chaps, looked like a puffy-faced beast. The man in brown duck had a new .30 caliber Krag-Jorgensen bolt action carbine, his partner a rusty old Henry lever action .44. At the instant of their surprise, they were carrying their rifles, not in their rifle boots, but out and slantwise across the inside of their saddleforks, hair trigger ready for a snapshot.

They weren't on a mission to check on him, Willet knew; they were on an assignment to murder him. To shoot him on sight.

The man with the new Krag-Jorgensen started to swing it upward, and Willet drew and shot him. He drew as he always drew, unconsciously, completely economically, as though he were reaching for a piece of pie.

The man's mount went into a small shy, cramming into his partner's mount. This one, the man in the hairy chaps, had his riflebutt almost to his armpit to draw his bead when Willet blasted him. He shot him twice. Hip-shooting riflemen didn't worry Willet too much, bead-drawing riflemen sure as hell did.

Willet inspected them. They were both dead, the one in brown duck face-up under his horse's belly, the other twisted sprawling on the earth, tangled in his stirrup; Willet untangled him.

He examined the horses. Each bore a brand of two intersecting five pointed stars, *Double Stars*. He took off the horses' bridles and bits, and hung them on their saddlehorns.

He stood motionless a moment and glared at the dead men in sultry rage.

He hadn't wanted this to happen.

He'd wanted to talk to them.

The sun had set, a pumpkin colored afterglow had come and gone through the dusty undergrowth, and dusk was falling when Willet left an edging of saplings and came out into a huddle of buildings on the stream bank. He recognized it as the village of Aspen Creek. He asked for a Mr. Morgenson at the saloon and was directed through the twilight to a half-house-half-cabin on the outskirts.

Morgenson, with his tight belly, and in his fringed leather shirt, was sunk into an easy chair on his tiny porch, working on a pair of spectacles with a bandanna, polishing, breathing, polishing. He set them on his nose as Willet came up, and stared. Willet got down, hitched to an iron ring stapled into a tree, and said politely, "Remember me?"

"Yes," said Morgenson. He didn't seem to much care for the sight of Willet. "Come up and sit down."

Willet stepped onto the porch and sat himself a few feet away, on the head of a nailkeg. A few bird chirpings came from the black mass of cedar boughs overhead, but the creek behind them was silent; the frogs had already gone deep into their mud against the coming winter.

"I hear tell there was a killing up at Dakins Station the other night," said Morgenson.

"Is that so?" said Willet. "It must have happened after me and Mr. Lustrell left."

"What brings you back to Aspen Springs? I thought you'd be in Canada by now."

"I'm staying for the time being with the Lustrells at Winslow," said Willet. "We took a liking for each other."

Morgenson said nothing.

"I'm carrying a message to you, a request from Mr. Lustrell. He wants you to hide out Miss Lee down here for a while. Until things up yonder simmer down."

Morgenson took out a flat brownglass pint bottle, took a long gulp, wiped the bottlemouth with his sleeve, and thrust it at Willet.

Willet rejected it with a motion of his hand. He said, "I have reason to believe something pretty serious is going on up there at *Box L,* something that Mr. Lustrell doesn't know about."

"I got the same hunch," said Morgenson. "That's why I tried to get Shaw for him."

"They're trying to gun through a thimblerig of some kind on Mr. Lustrell," said Willet. "And they expect it to pay them a pile of money. I wish I knew what it was."

"I don't know, and I ain't sure I want to know."

"What give you the hunch in the first place?"

Morgenson heaved to his feet and went into the house. Inside, he lit a lamp. After a bit, he returned. He was holding an envelope.

Seating himself again, he said, "I was on a bench in the court square at Winslow one evening at dusk-dark, enjoying the cool breeze. They was a few people coming and going, but not many. Beckett, of the *Double Star,* was across the street at the trough, watering his saddle horse. Julian Craycroft, of *Box L,* come up to him and handed him a letter. Them two outfits is supposed to be bad friends."

Willet said nothing.

Morgenson went on in a flat voice: "Beckett spread open the envelope, took out the letter, read it, and put it in his pants pocket. He balled up the envelope and dropped it in the mud by the trough. He mounted and rode away. Craycroft watched him go, and then went into a saloon. I got up, lazied over, and got the empty envelope. This is it." He passed it to Willet.

Willet smoothed it out on the porch floor, in the lampshine from the door, and looked at it.

It was addressed to, *Mr. Thomas Lustrell, Box L Ranch, Winslow County, Montana.* In the upper lefthand corner, the return address said, *Keefer Slaughtering and Packing Company, St. Louis, Missouri.* This was a big company; Willet had heard of it frequently. This was printed. Beneath it, in script, was written,

Robt. Treadway, Vice Pres. This had been a personal letter from Mr. Treadway to Mr. Lustrell. It had come to *Box L* for Lustrell, and Craycroft had passed it along up the line. Whatever it was, Mr. Lustrell never saw it.

"Did you tell Mr. Lustrell about this?" asked Willet.

"No, I didn't."

"But he said you and him was like blood brothers."

"That's right. Like blood brothers. Even closer."

"But you didn't want to mix in and get hurt."

"That's no way to talk."

"What if I tell him?" said Willet.

"You tell him, any part of what I've just said, and I'll deny it," said Morgenson. He scooped up the envelope.

"Then why did you tell me?" said Willet.

"He needs help," said Morgenson.

"You don't care if *I* mix in and get hurt."

"Something's got to be did, and I've got lumbago," said Morgenson.

Willet mused a moment, then said, "Why would a big packing house like Keefer be writing a letter to a ranch like *Box L?*"

"I haven't the slightest idea," said Morgenson.

"Packing houses buy cattle."

"But not that way." Morgenson was genuinely bewildered.

"And besides," said Willet, "from what I

keep hearing over and over again, *Box L* doesn't have no cows to speak of. Why would they pick *Box L.?*"

"It don't make no sense at all," said Morgenson.

"They's ranches in Texas, and other places," said Willet, "that might be cattle shy on a certain nightfall, yet be loaded with them come the next daybreak, but Mr. Lustrell wouldn't mess with that goings-on."

"He sure wouldn't."

"But what about Parrish?" said Willet. "What if he's figuring on using *Box L* as the shop window for some of his hocus-pocus?"

"Packing houses don't make secret deals to buy stole stock," said Morgenson.

"Packing houses is made up of people," said Willet. "And people come in sundries."

"But the letter was to Tom Lustrell, and He's as honest as the day is long."

"The letter could have been just a feeler. Something that Parrish decided to pick up and use."

Willet waited, got no response from Morgenson, and said, "They tell me many a stole cow has found its way into the Little Belts, and the *Double Star* had the Little Belts for a backyard."

Morgenson said, "The miasma from the creek. I got to be getting inside. My lumbago is killing me."

Willet said, "What shall I tell Mr. Lustrell about Miss Lee?"

"Tell him that it would be wiser for him to keep her with him up there at Winslow, that Aspen Creek is too lawless," said Morgenson. "Tell him that as much as I want to, I can't see no way to accommodate her down here. Tell him to set his jaw, and face this thing eye to eye, and everything is going to be all right. The darkest hour is just before the dawn. Tell him my hopes and wishes go with him because him and me are the same as blood brothers!"

"But you aren't going to take the girl."

"Tell him circumstances make it impossible. He'll understand."

"He won't, but I do," said Willet. "Good night."

He took the old mule road past Dakins Station. The delapidated buildings were dark and shadowy at the roadside.

When he came to the railroad tracks Mr. Lustrell had mentioned, he turned down the trail along them, to his left, to the west. Winslow had to be northwesterly. After a bit, he hobbled his mare in some scrub, stretched out on the ground, and got a few hours' sleep. About ten next morning, he came to a little back country store where he bought four inch-thick slices of bologna and a hatful of crackers.

It was nine that night when he got back to town.

VII

Railroad Row was at the height of its evening activity. The windows of the dingy shops were dull gold with smoky lamplight. The people up and down the boardwalk, and in the store doorways, were mainly ranchers and farmers, finishing up their trip to town, occupied with grain and feed and equipment, or drunks and loafers just standing around watching them. There were no women in view. The women would be sitting around somewhere in the backs of more respectable stores, in the more respectable part of the town's business section, packages in their laps and on the floor by their ankles, waiting for their menfolk and the return home. The temperature was dropping a little; Willet could see his breath sometimes, and that was a sign of weather to come he didn't much care for. He pulled up, got down, and hitched before the Great Northern Hotel. Behind him, in the switchyard, engines were grunting and clanking.

A chubby man in denims came forward to meet him, walking briskly. Willet exclaimed, "Why, Mr. Meacham. Good evening, sir."

The hide-buyer spoke quietly and rapidly. He said, "I'm going to tell you this, and then I'm going back to my office. Should you want to talk to me, you'll find me there. You see that paunchy little critter down the walk, whispering to Murray Parrish? That's Bill Dorfmann, the sheriff. He come to town some time back with Beckett and Parrish. Go up to him and say, 'Did you want to speak to me?' "

"Why would a sheriff want to speak to *me?*" asked Willet.

Hush-voiced, urgently, Mr. Meacham said, "Don't argue. Do it. Now!" And then Mr. Meacham was gone. His nauseating aroma of wet hides went with him.

Dorfmann and Parrish were standing on the boardwalk in the fall of windowlight from a harness shop, stooping slightly toward each other, conversing earnestly, when Willet joined them. They made an ugly-looking pair. Parrish, speaking softly, harshly, was laying out some kind of orders. Willet said, "Did you want to speak to me, Sheriff?"

They went rigid, and turned toward him slowly.

"That's him," said Parrish.

"Let's all take it easy now," said the sheriff.

"Well, did you or didn't you?" asked Willet.

"Who are you?" asked the sheriff.

"Name is Brady Willet," said Parrish. "I'm sometimes called Arizona, or Little Arizona."

The Arizona and Little Arizona part Willet had told nobody but Craycroft. He'd made it up out of thin air on the spur of the moment.

"What brings you to Winslow?" asked the sheriff menacingly.

"I'm on my way through," said Willet.

"Little Arizona," mused the sheriff. "Little Arizona. I think I got a dodger on you."

"I think you don't," said Willet.

"It's being said around town that you're a gun-thrower come here to make trouble," said the sheriff.

"Well, I ain't," said Willet.

"Then who are you?"

"Nobody."

"That ain't no answer," said the sheriff.

"It's the painful truth," said Willet. "Nobody."

"We don't want no undesirables in Winslow," said Sheriff Dorfmann. "And gun-throwers is considered undesirables."

"They should be," said Willet.

"You know what I think?" said Murray Parrish. "I think he's resisting questioning."

Resisting questioning, thought Willet, *That's a new one.* Resisting arrest, yes, but resisting questioning? You could kill a man for resisting arrest. Why couldn't you kill him for "resisting questioning"?

And then Willet realized in black anger that had been their original idea, to shoot him down while he was walking along, maybe. And what would it be? Suspicious undesirable, resisting questioning. But Mr. Meacham had upset their applecart.

They stared at him speculatively.

Almost inaudibly, Willet said, "If you got anything on your mind, try it. I'm passably good at self-defense."

Parrish said, "There's more than one way to skin a cat. Let's go, Sheriff." He wasn't scared, he was just using good judgment.

They walked away.

Turning on his heel, Willet headed in the opposite direction, toward Mr. Meacham's office. He passed the Judith River Café and glanced inside. There was a new fry cook behind the counter, a rosy-faced youngster who looked mighty fresh from the plow. When he came to the high board fence, he opened the double door, closed it behind him, and crossed the dark stinking yard to the little ramshackle office. He knocked, was called inside, and entered. Mr. Meacham was sitting by a lamp on the desk, drinking beer from a chipped fluted jelly glass. Another glass was on the desktop, waiting for Willet. Also on the desktop, handy, was a small lard bucket with lager in it. This was Mr. Meacham's "can." The "can," Willet knew, was the container a townsman took to a saloon for his draft beer for home use. Some mighty strange "cans" had been set down on mahogany bars, Willet had heard, scrubbed axle grease pails, cookie jars, empty carpet tack cannisters, crockery buttermilk pitchers, just about anything. Willet sat down.

Mr. Meacham poured him a jelly glass of amber liquid, scraped off the head with a penholder, and said, "Take this and forget your woes."

Willet took it and drank. He said, "Thank you for saving me, Mr. Meacham. Sheriff Dorfmann was all set to kill me, all right. When I was off guard sometime. For resisting questioning."

"Wonderful Winslow," said Mr. Meacham, reaching for his bucket. "Paradise on earth."

Willet settled back in his chair and gave the hide-buyer a long troubled stare.

Finally, he said, "Mr. Meacham, I don't want to drag you into something dangerous by even talking to you about it. But I sure as hell would like your opinion on something."

"My opinion on anything ain't worth much, son," said Mr. Meacham. "I'm a stupid mortal. But I'd be glad to listen to your worries."

Willet began to talk. He told him about his visit to the *Box L*, and the *Double Star*, and how Craycroft had to be in some kind of cahoots with Beckett and Parrish.

This was new information to Mr. Meacham, and he didn't like it. He took a swig of beer, blew his lips like a horse, and said, flat-voiced, "Poor Tom Lustrell."

Now Willet told him about his journey down

to the village of Aspen Creek, mentioning his visit with the Dunninghams, and the horseshoe nail, but omitting his encounter with the two riders.

Meacham said, "If they was parties trailing you, did they ever catch up with you?"

"I was making pretty good time," said Willet ambiguously, careful not to lie to a friend.

"They will," said Mr. Meacham.

"If so, I'll be ready," said Willet.

Then he told about his conversation with Morgenson.

Mr. Meacham listened motionless.

"My, my," he said.

"That's what I want your opinion on," said Willet. "On my way back I got to thinking. I can't believe it's the way I laid it out to him. It sounded like something while I was saying it, but I couldn't swallow it later when I thought it over. I mean Parrish bringing stole cows down from the northern ranches through the Little Belts into the *Double Star,* then moving them over onto *Box L,* and selling them."

"It couldn't be did in a hundred years," said Mr. Meacham. "Every *Box L* neighbor would know it. Cows is their business and their life, and they probably know *Box L* herds right now as well as Tom Lustrell. I doubt if a sick calf could be added, without them getting all excited over their supper table. And the shipping master at the railroad here in town would know it. A heap more folks know the number and condition of a man's cows than the owner. Par-

79

rish couldn't get away with nothing like that, even with Beckett's and Craycroft's kind assistance."

"But Parrish wants *Box L.*"

"He sure does."

"Then why?"

"I don't have no idea. It means money to him, someway. But I'd stake my life it ain't got nothing to do with stole cattle."

When Willet came up the garden walk of the Lustrell backyard, it must have been a little after eleven thirty. There was a light in the kitchen window, and this surprised him, for it was almost an eleventh commandment in this country that respectable people be abed at the stroke of nine. He stepped up onto the porch, and, where the curtains were parted a little, looked through. Three people were at the table, Miss Lee, Mr. Lustrell, and Craycroft. Craycroft. The *Box L* foreman-manager was talking earnestly, his arrogant face with its hard little eyes and cruel, tobacco-smeared lips, tense in the lampshine. Miss Lee was inspecting her fingernails. Mr. Lustrell was sipping coffee from a saucer, listening. Willet turned the china door knob, and walked into the room.

He shut the door softly behind him, and stood a moment, looking them over.

Craycroft said, "Since we last talked, I've found out who you really are. A gunhand."

"How could you find that out?" asked Willet.

"Every bartender and barber in town knows it," said Craycroft. "Mr. Lustrell and me won't be needing you no more. You can get on to Canada."

Puzzled, Willet said, "What is all this about?"

Miss Lee said, "Julian talked to Mr. Parrish on his own. Mr. Parrish agreed to a truce."

"How could there be a truce?" said Willet. "You folks haven't been doing nothing."

"He's agreed to take the pressure off," explained Mr. Lustrell.

"For what price?" said Willet.

"For no price," said the girl. "Just peace and tranquility."

Willet stood quietly. His face looked drawn and sinister.

"I'm trying to out-think him," he said finally. "And he's a hard man to out-think."

"What is it you don't like?" asked Mr. Lustrell.

Willet said, "I never much cared for truces. They's been many a man staked out and eat by ants in Yaqui truces down in Chihuahua."

"Nevertheless, that's it," said Mr. Lustrell. "I've always got to think of my daughter."

"You're right, Mr. Lustrell," said Craycroft. "We got to think of the girl."

"You mean you're finished with me?" said Willet. "And you're putting me out?" His tone was very mild.

Mr. Lustrell was genuinely appalled. He said, "What a terrible idea! You're our friend.

We'd like you here as long as you can stay."

"I'd think twice about that-there," warned Craycroft. "Mr. Parrish has took a personal dislike to him."

To Mr. Lustrell, Willet said, "I seen the party you asked me to see. He says to tell you that circumstances makes it impossible."

"What's this?" said Craycroft. "What are we talking about?"

To Willet, Mr. Lustrell said, "Thanks. The way things have worked out in the meantime, we don't need it."

"Don't need what?" asked Craycroft.

"I think I'll go to bed," said Willet.

"I'll bring you in an onion-omelet sandwich and a glass of milk," said the girl. "You must be hungry after your trip. How would that be?"

"That would be mighty nice," said Willet.

VIII

It was maybe a half an hour later when she came with the food. He was sitting on the edge of his bed, alert, listening, when he heard her approaching footsteps outside. He made it out into the hall before she got there, took the tray from her hands, thanked her, got back inside and got the door bolted in a hurry. There was sweat on his forehead. He was afraid she would edge her way in before he could stop her. He had been told that no decent woman ever came into a man's bedroom, even for harmless purposes, and he was bound and determined to keep her reputation spotless. The night she had come in, the night she had first showed the room to him, he hadn't known what to say or do—but he certainly sure wasn't going to let it happen again. She'd looked at him pretty funny when he'd grabbed the tray and run, and had put it down probably that he was brainsick with hunger, but that was all right with him. The hell with being raised rough like he had been was that sometimes you had to make a fool of yourself protecting innocent people against their innocence.

He had just finished eating and had taken off his boots when there was a knock. Mr. Lustrell called "Can I come in?" and Willet called back "Yes, sir."

Mr. Lustrell came in and sat on a chair. Willet asked, "Mr. Craycroft gone?"

"Just left," said Mr. Lustrell. "And he sure tried to set me against you."

"Sorry to hear it," said Willet. "But as you wend your way through life, you got to put up with a lot of such-like."

"How did your trip to Aspen go?"

"I went down by way of the creek path and come back by way of Dakins Station and the railroad tracks," said Willet, avoiding any detail.

"Anything interesting happen?" asked Mr. Lustrell.

"Yes, sir," said Willet. "I had noon dinner with a mighty fine family named Dunningham."

"I know them by reputation," said Mr. Lustrell. "And what a reputation."

"They suited me okay," said Willet comfortably. "They're trash and I'm trash. They gave me a horseshoe nail." After a moment, he asked, "What's this about a so-called truce?"

"Parrish summoned Mr. Craycroft to him and told him. Mr. Craycroft brought the news to me. That's all I know. I could hardly believe it."

"Neither can I," said Willet.

Mr. Lustrell said, "I won't have to worry about Lee anymore."

"Wonderful," said Willet. "If true." He looked sour.

"One minute you're living on borrowed time," said Mr. Lustrell, and then, presto, it's all over. Peace. You're safe."

Willet suddenly looked at him intently. He was working the conversation around to something.

"Naturally, I had to cinch it," said Mr. Lustrell.

"Well, well," said Willet, cold and restrained. "And how did you cinch it?"

"We were living on borrowed time, Lee and me," said Mr. Lustrell.

"You said that before. How did you cinch it?"

"I thought if Parrish could make a move toward peace, so could I."

"What in the hell are you talking about, peace? You haven't been shoulder-shooting and chain-whipping *him*."

So I told him I'd consider selling him *Box L*."

"I'm leaving tomorrow morning," said Willet in suppressed fury. "Thank you for all you've did for me."

"You've got to be sensible about things like this," said Mr. Lustrell. "I got more land than I can look out after."

"Tell Miss Lee I said goodbye," said Willet.

Mr. Lustrell got up. His shoulders slumped, his face had sort of caved in, sort of gone to pieces. Willet glanced aside. It was hard to see a broken man. He looked at the floor.

He heard Mr. Lustrell leave, mutely. He heard the door open and softly shut.

He sat there for maybe a half hour in the silent house, thinking it over, this way and that, back and forth, trying to be sure the thing he'd decided on was the right thing to do, and couldn't come to any other decision. Get out, get going on his way again, and forget he'd ever been to a place called Winslow. And the sooner he started, the better. Her could be well on his way and lost to them forever before they began rustling around for breakfast. He stripped to the waist and shaved—he didn't know when he might have another chance— sponged his chest and arms with a wet wash-cloth—he was dog-tired—then dressed and put out the lamp. He raised the window again, and again let himself out into the sideyard.

Miss Lee was standing under the tree, in the grass among the windfall apples, waiting for him. She really startled him.

He said, "Don't never do nothing like that again!" A little more calmly, he said, "These are perilous times. Get in the house."

She said, "You're leaving?"

He said, "You never spoke truer words!"

"Why?" she asked.

"I'm just excess baggage now. Nobody here needs me no more. Parrish has finally worked his will on your father. Your father has give in to him. Parrish is pacified. Mr. Lustrell has told him he'd sell *Box L* to him."

"He told him he'd consider selling."

Angry, Willet remained silent.

The girl said, "What Papa really meant, I think, was that he'd consider possibly selling."

"Let's hope not," said Willet. "You don't talk to a man like Parrish that way."

"And why shouldn't we sell?" she said. "We got plenty of land."

"You too," he said.

"We were drowning. We had to have money, any kind, frantic bad."

"If I was drowning," said Willet, "and someone threw me a rope, and shook a pistol in my face, and said, 'Grab that, gol'blast you, that-there's a order,' I wouldn't touch it. I'd lay back and drown. I don't care for pistols in my face, and I don't care for orders."

She said desperately, "Can't you see, Brady? I'm out of my wits with terror. Please stay."

"Yes'm," he said. "I'll stay."

She began to cry.

He said, "Know anything about your father's business?"

"Everything," she said, getting herself under control. "I keep his books and all."

"Ever have any dealings with the Keefer

Slaughtering and Packing Company, of St. Louis?"

"Never. We don't have many cows. What we sell, we sell to jobbers here in Winslow. Of course, some of the big packers like Keefer have their special buyers out here, but we've never dealt with them."

"Ever have any business with their vice president, a gentleman named Mr. Robert Treadway?"

"No."

"Ever have any letters from him?"

"No. And I handle all the mail."

"Now you get back inside the house," Willet said.

She left. He waited for her window light to come on.

Somebody hit him behind the ear with a gun, flatly, barrel and cylinder. His skull seemed to burst in agony. He went to the ground. He fought his way wildly to one knee, half erect, and he was hit again. His eyeballs seemed curdled milk and fire sparkles, and he fought this, too, trying to stay conscious, trying to keep his vision. They were on him now, manhandling him, wrenching his arms behind him, and they felt like a hundred and ten men. There was the smell of popskull whiskey fuming close to his face, and sweat, and the odor of workboots reeking with neat's-foot oil leather dressing. There were too many for him. As he twisted and fought, fists of rockhard knuckles slammed him again and again to subdue him.

Then Mr. Lustrell got into the picture.

He leaped through the back door onto the back porch in a lunge. He was in pants and undershirt, and his suspenders, off of his shoulders, looped down to his knees. In one hand he held a fiery little bundle, Miss Lee's kitchen apron, rolled, kerosene soaked and blazing, and in the other a heavy two-barreled elk gun. He tossed the torch in their direction, where it fell, flaming.

"Now we got some light!" he yelled.

The night under the appletree was turned into a cave of stark illlumination.

Foggy, dazed, Willet got to his feet.

The men were gone.

"Five of 'em." said Mr. Lustrell, coming up to him. "They sure decamped, didn't they?"

"I'd decamp, too," said Willet, "if I was elk gun threatened." When he got his breath, he asked, "Did you see who they were?"

"*Double Star* hands," said Mr. Lustrell. "I've saw most of them some time or other. What's that you've got hanging from your left hand?"

Willet raised his wrist. There was a narrow whang of rawhide, a couple of feet long, clove hitched to his thumb just below the first joint. "They were trying to tie my hands behind me," he said. "Indian style tying."

"But why?"

"They wanted to take me someplace and ask me questions, I'd say," said Willet.

"At least they didn't kill you on sight."

"Which might have been best, if it hadn't been for you," Willet said. "I don't want nobody who knows how to hand-tie Indian style asking me no questions."

"I'm going back to bed," said Mr. Lustrell. "And you'd better get some sleep, too. For your trip."

"I ain't taking no trip, not just now," said Willet. "I had me a change of mind."

"Well, now that's wonderful news," said Mr. Lustrell, beaming. Wait until Lee hears that at breakfast."

"Yes, sir," said Willet.

"I was half undressed when I heard the goings-on out here," said Mr. Lustrell. "I learned that fireball trick from my daddy, who learned it in the old days. It was pretty good on ranches, when you woke up in the night and heard thieves messing around outside."

"Well, I'll never forget it," said Willet. "And you can bet on that. Mr. Lustrell, did you ever have any transactions, any at all, with Keefer Slaughtering and Packing Company of St. Louis?"

"Not as far as I know. Sometimes stock is sold, and maybe resold, and maybe resold again before it winds up in a packing house yard somewhere. So I can't swear to where any of my cows ended up. But I, personal, have never had no business with them."

Ever have any dealings with a Mr. Robert Treadway?"

"No."

"Never met him?"

"No."

"Or received any letters from him?"

"Never even heard of him. Who is he supposed to be?"

Willet said, "Mr. Lustrell, you just saved me, and I'm deeply beholden to you, which makes it worse, but I've got to know for sure. Are you talking to me straight? Are you telling me the truth?"

Serious, but unoffended, Mr. Lustrell said, "I'm telling you the truth."

"Then I don't know what from what," said Willet. "Someway, we're being outfoxed."

"Something I've been wondering about," said Mr. Lustrell. "What in the hell are you doing out here in the first place?"

"Very easy to explain," said Willet, thinking hard for an explanation.

One thing certain, he wasn't going to mention Miss Lee, and her crying at all. Fathers always thought the worst.

"I was getting me a windfall apple," said Willet. "I dearly enjoy a big old juicy winesap."

They walked toward the house.

Willet thought about the men who had just tried to take him away. A couple of hours ago, the word had been for the sheriff to shoot him. But now, through Craycroft likely, they knew he'd just come back from a trip, and wanted to know the details. Willet had seen men play checkers this way, starting to make a move, worrying, pausing, starting to make another move instead, worrying, making it, still worrying. There must be a lot at stake in this particular checker game, he decided.

As they stood in the downstairs hall by his bedroom door, Mr. Lustrell said, "You're walking a little game-leg, son. They hurt you bad?"

"Nothing wrong with me," said Willet. "Just a little stiff."

Miss Lee came flying up to them in her dressing robe. She looked lovely. "Are you all right, Mr. Willet?" she asked tautly.

"I'm fine," said Willet.

Now it was Mr. Willet.

Out there, when she thought he was going away, she'd called him Brady.

Sometimes there was no rhyme or reason to a female.

Why couldn't they act and think and talk like everybody else?

IX

Next morning, the breakfast taste of Lustrell pancakes and plum jam still in his mouth, Willet walked down Railroad Row, heading for the depot. He passed mangy dogs, a few scrawny scavenger cats, a few shopkeepers sweeping their walks for the day's business, but saw neither Parrish, nor the sheriff, nor any sign of *Box L* or *Double Star*. Once, he passed a hitched claybank gelding that bared its teeth at him in a good-natured pretense at viciousness, and Willet bared his teeth right back. When he came to the watch repair shop with the heavy woven-wire window grille, he went down two squared logs at the sidewalk's edge and crossed the rough wheelcut road to the depot. He walked in, sent a telegram, paid for it, and walked out.

The telegram he'd sent said:

Keefer Slaughtering and Packaging Company, St. Louis, Missouri. Have good reason to believe that an important letter sent to me here in Winslow, Montana, by your vice president, Mr. Robert Treadway, was lost someway at this end before it could be delivered. Would appreciate it very much if you would tell me what it said. Thanks, Tom Lustrell, Winslow, Montana.

The man behind the counter had told him that the service to St. Louis was topnotch, and the answer would come through that day. Willet had said to hold the answer, as Mr. Lustrell would send him to pick it up later.

He was sure they would be glad to handle it. That was the way big companies got big. And he'd heard they always kept copies of letters they sent; in his father's day in letter-books, now in special little cupboards and drawers.

A few vehicles were moving around now, several wagons, a grocery dray or two, a bakery dray. He recrossed the road, mounted the logs, and started down the boardwalk. The switchyard, too, was increasing its activity. Engines were chuffing and grinding, and bells were glong-glonging.

Something had been nagging at his mind. At first he couldn't pin it down, and then he finally did. That big claybank gelding that had gone through the playful mouth-motions of biting him. He'd seen the animal before, somewhere. He couldn't be wrong. Horses had a magic for him. Any horse, even a half starved mustang colt, was big medicine to him.

He'd seen that gelding on the night he'd gone to *Box L*, and Craycroft had been riding it.

He speculated on what could have possibly brought the foreman-manager to town so early in the day, and decided to look into the matter.

He'd passed the gelding where it had been tied before a vacant lot. Now, when he got there, it was gone. He began a systematic search of streets, sidestreets, and backstreets. He found the claybank some distance away, on a run-down backstreet, before a corner shop with the sign: Cigars. It was a dingy miserable-looking shop and in its single show window were a secondhand filthy mattress and a rack of rusty broken-down rifles and shotguns, with a card saying, *For Sale*. The claybank was hitched at a rail with four other horses.

That was a notable amount of horses for a wretched little out-of-the-way place like this before noon. Not sensational, but sizable and interesting. The place *could* be a kind of hangout.

For Parrish's group? Why not? A smart man like Parrish would pick a place like this, and not his Great Northern Hotel, as a kind of undercover headquarters. The assembly of horses didn't have to mean that something was getting ready to explode; it could mean that a few pals had dropped in to while away a little time. It likely happened all day long.

Willet went inside. A small group of men

were gathered by a glass cigar showcase, talking, gossiping. When they saw him, they fell dead silent. He could hear his own bootsteps and the clinking of his spurs as he approached them.

They were tough-looking, and returned his inspection of them with open hostility. The proprietor, a chinless man with dull limestone eyes, came forward belligerently. In a hoarse insulting tone, he asked, "Well, what do you want?"

"Maybe I want to buy me a dirty mattress," said Willet. "You should speak nice to strangers."

Craycroft wasn't in sight.

Willet scanned the brutal faces. He wondered how many, if any, had been in the party that had slammed him around the night before in the Lustrell sideyard.

One of them spoke to him. He said, "You heard the man. What do you want? Take care of your business and be on your way."

Willet turned soft eyes to him. He said, "I had a bad night. I wouldn't advise nobody monkeying with me unless he should mean it."

They subsided so quick it was pitiful to see.

In a way, he was sorry.

At the back of the room was a short broad hall, with two doors at either side and one at the end. Back there were living quarters for the owner, probably, Willet thought. The end door opened. Parrish came in from the back lot. He came down the hall and entered a room at the side. He moved as though he knew where he was going, as though he had been there before. The door panel swung shut behind him.

Willet brushed through the cluster of men, went down the hall, opened the door without knocking, and stepped inside.

He found himself in the owner's bedroom-sitting room. There was a double-decked barracks bunk along one wall, its lower bed neatly made up and turned back, tis upper bed used as a bachelor's storage shelf, stacked with cardboard boxes, brown paper sacks, and wads of soiled clothes. On the opposite wall there was a large beer company poster of the Fetterman massacre at Fort Kearny. In the middle of the room, two men sat on straightbacked chairs, facing each other across a red painted packingbox table—Craycroft and Parrish. On the table, between them, was a drawstring money pouch, open, and a couple of hundred dollars in gold double eagles.

Craycroft's hand was above the money. When he saw Willet, he became immobile, then put his empty hand in his lap.

"Go right ahead, pick it up," said Willet. "Don't pay no mind to me. I'm just ambling around looking for a lost dog name of Old Bigtooth. He been in here?"

Parrish got up, wordlessly, stiffly, and headed for the door.

As he passed Willet, Willet said, " 'Morning, Mr. Parrish. Did any of your friends bring you back any of Mr. Lustrell's tasty winesaps last. night?"

Parrish seemed stone deaf.

When he had gone, Craycroft said, "Sit down, Willet."

"Why not?" said Willet, and sat down.

Craycroft said, "Having a good time? You know what Mr. Parrish's trade was before he came here?"

"I don't figure it would be too hard to track down," said Willet. "Probably what people are trying to lay on me—gunman."

"The best."

"It's funny thing about gun artists," said Willet. "It perishes the brain to try to reason it out, but it's a fact. They ain't no best. Some is a heap better'n others, and likewise the opposite, but they ain't no best. They all run into the wrong man sometime. It's sort of a confusing law of nature."

Craycroft said, "You like the look of that money there on the table?"

"I always like the look of money," said Willet.

"Then drag out three of them coins, sixty dollars, and put 'em in your pocket."

"No," said Willet. "I don't need them. By chance, I'm sufficiently fixed at present."

"Lustrell's money?"

"Correct."

"I was told to ask you a question," said Craycroft. "And I hope for your sake you'll answer it. What carried you down to Aspen Creek the other day?"

They'd tracked the horseshoe nail as far as Dunningham's. From there on, they'd have to guess. They knew about the dead riders.

"I went to Dunningham's," said Willet. "I didn't go on down to the village. I was carrying a request to them from Mr. Lustrell."

"What message, may I ask?" said Craycroft, trying to sound offhand.

"I don't see why I shouldn't tell you," said Willet. "There wasn't nothing private or personal about it. Mr. Lustrell wanted Mr. Dunningham to jerky him some beef for his hands for winter fenceline riding, but Mr. Dunningham said due to circumstances it was impossible. Mr. Dunningham's mighty busy at the moment, hustling around, trapping the last of the turtles before the freeze."

"It tries my soul just to listen to you," said Craycroft.

"I feel the same way," said Willet.

Craycroft took out his watch and looked at it. "Well, it's done by now," he said smugly. He turned the dial toward Willet. It was eleven o'clock.

"What's done now?" said Willet. "What do you mean?"

"Tom Lustrell has sold the *Box L* to Mr. Parrish. And I got me a new boss."

Willet went rigid. "That couldn't be!"

"It's the truth."

"But Mr. Lustrell told me he was considering," said Willet.

"And by now he's considered," said Craycroft. "Maybe he forgot to tell you there was a time limit set. Eleven this morning."

"Where are they handling this, where?"

"At the Great Northern Hotel bar. And it's a

good thing for the girl," said Craycroft. "Mr. Parrish was beginning to turn against her, beginning to blame her for her old man's stubbornness."

Willet left. Fast.

There it was, he thought when he got to it, Murray Parrish's Great Northern R.R. Hotel with its blistered green-painted clapboard and moldy rain barrels—the spawning nest of grief and tribulation. Just left of the lobby door was another, with a sheet of paper tacked to it: *Free Lunch Today, Fried Tripe & Pickles*. This would be the door to the bar. You mainly found free lunches in deluxe bars, or bars specializing in steady, long session drinkers. The profit on one beer wouldn't pay for a piece of tripe, but the profit on four would, and over. He went inside. It was deluxe.

The room was low-ceilinged, square, and dim. To his right as he entered was a doorway with the door removed, and before it a big straw matting screen; this would lead to the lobby and the hotel. There were several customers, townsmen, at the walnut veneer bar, and the fat barman behind it was amusing them playing odd-man-out with them with pennies. There were about ten tables—empty; the noon assembly of merchants wouldn't begin drifting in for about an hour. The bar was waxed until it shone, and any glassware in sight sparkled enough to take the skin off of your eye. About two-thirds of the way down the room was a white lattice, about as high as a man's head, woven in and out with artificial flowers in pink muslin, with a gate in it. Lattices were high-toned since the big fair at St. Louis. This lattice was the deluxe to the place. There must be a women's wineroom behind it, Willet decided, which meant a more private entrance to it also, a side door back there. No woman would walk through the bar, of course, even a parlor-house girl, with men looking at her from behind after she'd passed.

He went to the lattice, opened the gate, and stepped into the wineroom beyond it.

It had been cleared of customers. A group of men, Mr. Lustrell, several cowboys in leather and brass town finery, Parrish, Beckett and Craycroft, stood in a circle over a man seated at a little round-topped ice-cream parlor table. Miss Lee was there, too, and that was why, Willet realized, the assembly was being held in the ladies' section of the bar. She was dressed attractively in coffee colored autumn wool, and looked mighty subdued. Mr. Lustrell looked cold and strained. Parrish and Beckett were smiling, as the oldtimers used to say, like cats eating paste. This was only the second time Willet had seen Beckett, and took a good long stare at him; with that gaunt hunched-over posture, and those slimy rotten teeth, he looked mighty hardcase. Craycroft managed to give off the feeling that nothing was happening, or going to happen, that he was just standing around wasting his time.

Mr. Lustrell nodded at Willet as he came up,

unsmiling. The others ignored him. He could almost feel their hatred for him in the air. Mr. Lustrell said, "Howdy, Brady, and welcome. Most of us you know. The gentleman at the table is Parson Waterfield, a notary. Mr. Parrish brought him here. Parson, Mr. Willet."

Willet liked the looks of him. He was a gnarled little man, threadbare, with honest, steely eyes. In front of him were papers, printed legal forms, a black cast iron notary seal that worked up and down like a cheeseknife, a bottle of ink, a penholder and pen, and a much used chamois penwiper. He returned the introduction with a nod, and said, "Pleased to meet you. Mr. Parrish didn't *bring* me here. I'm here because he said I'd be needed."

"Now that we're all in convention convened, including strays and drifters," said Parrish, "let's get this finished up."

He took a certified check from a morocco wallet as big as a Bible, and pushed it at Mr. Lustrell.

Mr. Lustrell made no movement to accept it.

"You were given until eleven to consider," said Parrish. "The Seth Thomas there on the wall says seven after."

"I've considered," said Lustrell. "And decided not to sell."

There was an apoplectic silence.

"Then you won't need me after all," said Parson Waterfield, gathering together his paraphernalia.

"Stay where you are!" ordered Parrish viciously. "We ain't through yet. I ain't prepared to take that no of his. Was it Willet, here, Mr. Lustrell, that turned your thinking?"

"It was you and *Double Star*," said Mr. Lustrell. "My home, wherever I am, is private to me. I won't stomach what happened in its sideyard last night."

"What was that?" asked Parrish.

"A bunch of your *Double Star* riffraff come in and tried to mayhem me and the boy here," said Mr. Lustrell, deliberately, and a little untruthfully, putting himself as a part-target of the action.

"Why would they do that?" asked Parrish woodenly.

"Trying to put the fear of God in me, I guess," said Lustrell. "Trying to make double sure I'd sell. All it come to was to make sure I wouldn't. You should have studied my nature a little more close before you done a thing like that."

Turning to Beckett, Parrish asked, "Is this true?"

"Don't take that tone to me, you third-rater," said Beckett. "This is a good a time as any to tell you that you've always been a stink to my nostrils."

"Mr. Lustrell," said Parrish, "what makes you think they were *Double Star* men?"

"I know all of 'em to nod to," said Mr. Lustrell, "and some well enough to call by name."

"Call 'em by name for me," said Parrish.

Mr. Lustrell clamped his jaw and said nothing.

To Beckett, Parrish said, "I believe him. What were you up to? Why do I always get saddled with idiots?"

"Watch it, Murray," said Beckett, backing to one side, out into the open.

"And about being a third-rater," said Parrish musingly. "Let's find out."

Beckett's fingers went down for his gunbutt, and Parrish shot him.

He shot him dead center in the heart with three cartridges that burned so close together they seemed like one flaming cough. It took a special gun action—one that had been altered, and home doctored, and much babied—to do that, Willet knew. Parrish hadn't even seemed to draw, seemed to shoot; there was just the noise and smoke. And his gun was back in its holster. His face was relaxed. That was the way you spotted a real professional. Afterward, Beckett was on the floor—as though he'd been dumped there, lifeless, from a sack.

Craycroft blew out his breath. "That was a close one, Mr. Parrish," he said.

"What do you think, Parson?" asked Parrish.

"Self-defense," said Parson Waterfield.

"Mr. Lustrell?" asked Parrish.

"Self-defense," said Mr. Lustrell.

"And you, Miss Lustrell?" said Parrish.

Miss Lee hesitated. "It happened so quick," she said.

The cowboys mumbled self-defense.

"And now," said Parrish. "We come to the expert. The gun tramp himself. What is your judgment, Mr. Willet?"

"He had it in his mind to kill you, if that's what you mean," said Willet. "Further than that, I don't care to discuss it."

"Why not?" said Parrish.

"A rat can have it in his mind to gnaw through a cast iron stove," said Willet. "But doing so is a different matter."

Parrish said, "Mr. Lustrell, because of the little misunderstanding, I'm giving you a postponement. Let's say same time tomorrow, right here again. Go home and smooth yourself out. All right with you, Parson? Good."

Lustrell and Miss Lee just stood there, looking stunned.

Parrish said, "I've never give nobody a postponement before, and certainly sure never will again."

He, Craycroft, and cowboys left. Parson Waterfield followed them.

Miss Lee said, "Let's go home. Our noonday dinner is waiting for us. We're going to have beef stew and cornmeal dumplings."

Mr. Lustrell said, "He wouldn't, couldn't have butchered his own foreman just as a lesson to me."

"He would, but I don't know if he did," said Willet. "Things are moving mighty fast."

The barman came running in from the front, his customers trailing behind him.

A smart barman waited until it was all over. He was paid to serve drinks.

X

They walked home slowly, talking. Mr. Lustrell was back again to where he'd been before. Scared. Scared for Miss Lee. Willet was scared for her, too, but was careful not to upset them by showing it.

At one end of the Lustrell front porch a piece of wire fencing, chickenwire with little interstices, had been nailed from the cornices under the eave gutters to the foundation beams just above the ground; it was now hung with snarls of dying, frostbitten eglantine. Behind it, where you could sit and look at people, and people couldn't look at you, was a slatted porch swing, its cushions already taken in by Miss Lee for the winter. As they came up on the porch, a man arose from the swing and intercepted them. It was Craycroft. "Julian!" said Mr. Lustrell, distressed.

One eye, half open, had a mouse under it. One cheek, red and hammered-looking, had a deep crimson scratch on it. It looked mighty like a gunsight gouge to Willet.

"What happened to you, Julian?" asked Mr. Lustrell.

"I was trying to give a hand to a farmer loading a wagon, and a harrow slipped on me," said Craycroft.

"It bears an interesting resemblance to a pistol-whipping," said Willet. "Did Mr. Parrish do that to you?"

"When I want your opinion, I'll ask for it," said Craycroft. He turned to Mr. Lustrell. "Mr. Parrish made me a proposition."

"You're not in a position to accept any propositions from Parrish," said Mr. Lustrell. "You draw your wages from me."

"I may be. In the near future. When you sell," said Craycroft.

"What was this proposition?" asked Miss Lee.

Craycroft said, "A kind of joint managership of both the *Double Star* and the *Box L.*"

"What did you tell him?" asked Miss Lee.

"At first I told him no," said Craycroft.

"What do you mean, at first?" said Willet.

"He finally argued me into it."

"You show it," said Willet.

"And you came here to tell us?" said Miss Lee.

"Yes," said Craycroft. "After you sell, and if I should turn up running both outfits, I didn't want you to be surprised and bear me no ill will. I wanted you to understand."

"You know something?" said Willet. "Your one man, Mr. Craycroft, I'll never forget."

"How come?" asked Craycroft suspiciously.

"You're the only man I ever met who got himself pistol-whipped into a promotion," said Willet.

Craycroft went down the walk to the street, and up the street.

He hadn't said goodbye.

Miss Lee said, "Why is a farmer loading a harrow this time of year?"

"Let's get inside," said Mr. Lustrell. "And get to work on some of that cornmeal dumplings and stew."

A little after eight that night, Willet returned to the depot, to see if answer had come to his telegram to St. Louis. An answer had come, all right. The autumn night was black and crisp. Nothing had happened along Railroad Row. He'd expected nothing to happen. Parrish would be holding off at the moment, waiting. At the depot, there was a different man behind the counter, the night man, probably. Any town that was important enough to have a switchyard and a roundhouse would likely have a night man on the telegraph key. He was a pleasant nimble-looking little man in his seventies, with a pollen of yellow stubble on his jaw, and big round windowpane spectacles. After Willet had asked, the man said sure, it had come in a little while ago. He tore a page from a pad and handed it to Willet.

Willet read it:

Thomas Lustrell, Winslow, Montana. No information on your query Mr. Treadway's letter. This must have been Mr. Treadway's personal business. Mr. Treadway is not here but on vacation. Has left word he is going to Winslow, Montana. Took train 119 car Chevy Chase should you wish to contact him in transit. Keefer Slaughtering and Packing Company, St. Louis, Missouri.

"Coming to Winslow?" said Willet, stunned.

"That's what it says."

"Contact him in transit?"

"We can get telegrams to moving trains at points along the way."

"Well, I want to contact him in transit," said Willet.

"In this case, you can't," said the night clerk. "We don't know what line did he take out of St. Louis, or when did he leave. Even if we had that information, we don't know what changes he'd scheduled, and what lines he was changing to, and there's a multitude of lines and choices 'twixt here and St. Louis. Forget him while he's in transit and consider him lost. Even the good Lord has to consider him lost."

Willet left the waiting room, went out onto the laoding platform, and perched on the corner of a furniture crate. He was trying to work it out, wondering what he should do, when the night clerk came out and sat beside him. They sat for a moment in companionable silence, and then the old man said, "It'll be nice to see Mr. Treadway again."

Startled, Willet said, "You know him?"

"Nice fellow," said the oldster. "He raises fantail pigeons. Do you, by any chance?"

"No," said Willet, and almost held his breath.

"I do," said the man. "My, what good chats we had about 'em."

"When was he here?" asked Willet.

"Last autumn," said the man. "On vacation, like now."

"Where did he stay?" said Willet. "Did he happen to mention? At the Great Northern Hotel?"

"No, at Mrs. Mullen's Board-and-Room. I sent him there."

"Why did you send him there?" asked Willet.

"She raises fantails, too. I knowed they'd be mutually compatible."

"How do I find this place?" asked Willet.

The night clerk gave him detailed directions. Willet got up, nodded, and walked away.

From behind him, the station clerk yelled, "Her and me loans each other cockbirds."

Mrs. Mullen's Board-and-Room was a dilapidated, lopsided, three-story residence with a battery of lighted windows and a sign that said, BACHELOR RAILROAD GENTLEMEN OUR SPECIALTY, flush to the broken brick sidewalk, facing the roundhouse. Mrs. Mullen herself answered Willet's tugging at the bell cord. She had a blocky motherly face with dewlaps, coarse-grained and rice-powdered beneath the eyes, and was dressed in a white blouse with a high whalebone ribbed net collar (to hide her withered gullet) and a black skirt with a rosette of cut jet beads at her hip. She looked at him once, and said, "You been having it hard, haven't you, boy?"

Willet said, "I sure have."

She said, "You just follow me down this hall to the kitchen, and we'll put a little supper into you."

"I don't mean that way," said Willet. "I'm all right, that way. I was speaking generally. Mrs. Mullen, the night man at the depot told me you knew Mr. Robert Treadway of St. Louis. Is he here?"

"No, he isn't," she said. "But he was here last fall. And a very pleasant guest he was."

"What brought him away out here to this godforsaken place?"

"There's some of us that don't think it's godforsaken. The *Winslow Gazette* calls it the 'Heartland of Humanity.' You must be from Wyoming, or some of those outlandish places."

"Yes, ma'am, from the Chugwater. What brought him out here?"

"Ill health and weak lungs. He hired him a saddle horse and a packhorse, and camped over three counties."

"Looking them over?"

"Inhaling some of this marvelous doctor's-prescription ozone."

"I got information he's coming here again," said Willet.

"That's mighty fine news," said Mrs. Mullen. "I'll always have a room for him. Even if I have to give the bum's rush to Number Seventeen."

"What's wrong with Number Seventeen?" asked Willet, always interested in side issues.

"The feminine gender, and that's strictly prohibited," said Mrs. Mullen.

"You mean Number Seventeen brings in girls?"

"Worse than that. He brings one down from the attic—my hired girl. She's getting so she serves him the choice food, the kidney fat from the lamb, the fillets from the steaks, and suchlike."

Willet said, "You know where Mr. Tom Lustrell lives here in Winslow?"

"Yes, I do," she said. "Miss Lee contributes fondant to our church bazaars."

"If you see Treadway, would you tell him Mr. Lustrell wants to talk to him on a matter of importance?"

"I sure will. Miss Lee cooks up her fondant sugar, then beats it, then kneads it, then wraps it in a wet cloth and leaves it set all night on a marble slab. Next day, when she works in her extracts and coloring and shapes it, it's so smooth it's heavenly. You like bonbons?"

"I don't believe I ever saw any," said Willet. "Thank you, ma'am."

"You can find you some at almost any church bazaar."

"I'll remember that," said Willet. "Good night."

He was walking along the marqueed sidewalk, the busy switchyard with its shunting and puffing engines on his left, the row of low-grade cut-rate shops on his right, when he passed the high board fence of the Meacham hide-yards. Mr. Meacham in his stinking filthy pants, coatless, but wearing a big-armholed pinto ponyskin vest over two sweaters against the chill, was sitting on a thong-bottomed chair in front of his double gate. When Willet came up and stopped, he said, "Well, ain't nobody demised you yet, I see."

"Not yet, I'm glad to state," said Willet. "My hopes and aspirations are to the contrary."

"I'm pleased to see you," said Mr. Meacham. "I've been thinking about a little conversation that might interest you."

"All conversations interest me," said Willet. "Even how to make fondant."

"What's fondant?"

"How the hell should I know? It's something to eat, I think. You soak it all night in a wet rag."

"My mother used to call it cottage cheese. You take this clabber and drain the curds. It comes out looking like calf brains, but it ain't too bad."

"What was it you were fixing to say before

we got talking about calf brains?" said Willet.

Mr. Meacham said, "I was in the Emporium the other day. It's a monstrous two story general store on court square, everything from felt boots to pianos to female tonic. Ever drink any female tonic?"

"No," said Willet.

"I did once. It's like blasting powder, about a hundred and ten proof, I'd say. Can't no man handle it. Well, I was downstairs, at the back, in the harness section, looking for a new bridle buckle. Murray Parrish come in and stood beside me. He told his clerk he wanted three cheap working saddles for the *Double Star*, to be delivered out there."

Willet flinched. If you wanted a good saddle, you went to a saddlemaker you knew about, and if you wanted good harness, you went to a good harnessmaker. More valuable than anything, next to his gun, maybe, was a man's saddle; it had to be the best obtainable. Now, lately, they were sending in these cheap readymades from the East. More men were seriously hurt from cheap saddles than from gopher holes. Many a boy would rather inherit his father's wonderful but pitiful-looking saddle than his father's gold hunter-case watch.

Willet said, "There ought to be a law against them bargain out-country saddles."

"You're right," said Mr. Meacham. "But that isn't what I was getting to. He told the clerk to charge them to the Judith River Café, per usual."

"What's wrong with that?" said Willet. "He owns the Judith River Café."

"I mentioned it afterward to the clerk, who is sociable, and friendly to me, and the clerk said Parrish always charges to the café; sometimes it's the café that pays, sometimes the *Double Star*, sometimes the Great Northern Hotel. No matter what is bought."

"Parrish owns them all."

"Maybe. Maybe he don't own none of them. Maybe he's a company."

"Do you think for sure?" asked Willet, startled.

"They do it in Chicago and St. Louis and them places all the time," said Mr. Meacham.

"That lousy Judith River Café," said Willet. "The Judith River Café Company. What next?"

"It seems to be doing all right, I'd say," said Mr. Meacham. "It runs a ranch, a restaurant, and a hotel. That *we* know of. Maybe other things too."

"Mr. Meacham," said Willet, "how do I find a preacher by the name of Waterfield?"

"Parson Waterfield? Easy. You'll find him in his parsonage."

"And where might that be?"

"I'd better tell you, at that. Or you'll pass it by thinking it's a hencoop."

Mr. Meacham told him. When he'd finished, he said, "So you feel the need of a preacher?"

"It just come over me all of a sudden," said Willet.

"I hear that's the way it works," said Mr. Meacham respectfully. "In a slow gentle ferment. Like rye whiskey mash."

Willet nodded an amiable good night and walked away.

As he passed the Great Northern Hotel, he saw Craycroft's big claybank gelding at the rack. A man was untieing it, and preparing to lead it away.

Willet said, "That's Mr. Craycroft's horse. What are you doing with it?"

The man said, "I'm taking it to the livery barn."

"Mr. Craycroft spending the night in town, here at the hotel?" asked Willet.

" 'Spect so," said the man. "They didn't say. I'm just doing what Mr. Parrish told me."

Willet continued down the walk. He wondered what Parrish was putting Craycroft up to now. Whatever it was, you could be sure he was just rehashing and emphasizing some step in a plan he had already carefully worked out. That was the way Parrish moved—in carefully planned steps.

If Mr. Meacham was right—if it was a combine and Parrish was just its gun-thrower—it didn't really have to be managed from here in Winslow. It could be run from some place far away, say like from the Columbia Plateau country in Oregon, which was where Parrish was supposed to have come from.

Maybe if he looked up the Judith River Café, the *Double Star,* and the Great Northern Hotel, in Deeds and Records and suchlike at the courthouse, he could learn something. Probably not; folks that did slippery things had slippery ways of doing them.

The courthouse would be closed now, but maybe he could rouse somebody up. He had to give it a try. Now. This thing couldn't wait.

XI

There were three main east-west thoroughfares through Winslow, Railroad Row, Main Street, and, farther south, in the residential district, Elm Street. Willet had passed the courthouse several times. It was on the north side of Main Street, the near side, facing its square with the small brass muzzle loading relic cannon that would still be sometimes fired, Willet knew, at celebrations or important buryings. The courthouse would be dark now, except maybe for a light or two in its new one story brick wing, the jail.

Main Street was Winslow at first, and the buildings which gradually fronted it; then the town built south, toward what was now Elm. The railroad and the buildings which were Railroad Row, north of Main, came later.

Sandwiched between the back doors of Main

and the back doors of Railroad Row was a patch of terrain which Willet had never heard of, known to the local inhabitants sometimes as Rat Town, sometimes as The Gully.

Taking a shortcut, figuring to come up on the courthouse from the rear, Willet turned down and alley, went maybe fifty yards, and found himself in Rat Town.

The moon was high and big and white. The scene around him was incredibly squalid and desolate. Before him was a shallow, eroded ravine with a putrid-looking ribbon of a creek. On either weedy bank there was a scattering of shanties, some dark, some glimmering with feeble candlelight. Everywhere there was trash and litter. The rancid-smelling stream was half choked with it. In this little community of scavengers, Willet realized, trash was salvage, and salvage was sustenance. There was no one in sight. Main Street, he knew, must be only three or four hundred yards away, but it seemed three or four hundred miles. Inside the shacks, he knew, would be families and their treasures, piles of empty bottles—always negotiable, mounds of scrap metal, gunny sacks of little pieces of coal picked up painstakingly from between the ties of the railroad tracks. An old door had been placed over the gully as a footbridge.

He crossed it, pushed through brittle dead ironweed, and came to a small dark shack sided with ancient tin roofing over scrap lumber. It was shut tight, and padlocked.

As Willet approached it along the beaten path, a man came out into the open from behind its far side and stood, in a friendly attitude, blocking his way, about ten feet in fron of him. The man said, "Pardon me, sir, but what town is this?" He was unarmed.

"Winslow. Winslow, Montana," said Willet sociably.

Then he threw himself to the ground.

He remembered that voice. He'd only heard it once, but it had made him mad, and he'd never forget it.

He hit the ground and twisted. He knew that a trap had been triggered for him. And that his danger lay behind him.

The blackish shadow behind him, and a little to one side, half rising from a clump of scrub, seemed hardly a man, but the moonlight on it showed a tongue of bluish glint, gun metal from a drawn pistol. Willet shot to kill, and the figure went over and back.

That's the trouble with a trap, Willet thought bleakly; *if he doesn't mind his p's and q's, it can catch the man that tries to set it.*

Willet got up. Now the other man came forward, and he was exactly the one Willet had thought, the desk man Willet had talked to that morning at the Great Northern Hotel, the *hombre* with the ugly scabby jaw.

He said, "Don't shoot. I was forced into this. I don't have a weapon." His squeaky voice was so desperate that Willet almost felt sorry for him.

120

Together, they turned the dead man over. It was Murray Parrish.

"He's a professional, of course," said Willet.

"Yes, sir," said the desk man.

"A professional always hedges his risk," said Willet. "Backshooting suits a professional just dandy."

"Yes, sir," said the desk clerk.

The professional gunman, unlike the gunfighter, everybody knew, didn't put any stock in fairness. He had a job to take care of, and tried to take care of it with as little danger to himself as possible, so he could take care of the next one. Like a bricklayer or a blacksmith, it was a living.

Willet said, "I'm going to ask you a question, and if you're smart, you'll tell me the truth first time, because my temper happens to be a little short just about now. How come you all were here waiting for me?"

"Mr. Parrish seen you go into the alley. He knew you'd likely be taking this path. Me and him cut around ahead of you."

There were heavy footsteps as a man pounded up at a run.

It was Sheriff Dorfmann. "Who fired the shot?" he said.

"I did," said Willet. "I killed this man here."

The sheriff glanced toward the ground. "Murray Parrish!"

"That's right," said the hotel clerk. There was a relief in his voice, too. This Parrish must have been a mad dog, Willet decided.

"What happened?" asked the sheriff.

The hotel clerk said, "Mr. Willet here and me was walking along the path. Mr. Willet had run into me on Railroad Row and asked me could I show him where he might buy himself a cheap pair of secondhand chaps. I told him we could come back here and inquire around. These people might know. They specialize in secondhand. A man stood up out of this clump of brush with his shirt collar over the bridge of his nose and said, 'Brady Willet, now I got you,' and went for his gun and Mr. Willet shot him. We didn't know it was Murray Parrish then."

"You outdrew him, Mr. Willet?" said the sheriff skeptically.

"How do I know what I did?" said Willet. "I was scared out of my wits, all a-tremble."

"I bet," said Sheriff Dorfmann. "About like you are now."

Willet was revising his opinion of Sheriff Dorfmann. He was sure now that he was talking to a topnotch lawman. He was beginning to like him.

The sheriff said thoughtfully, "So Murray Parrish, like all them that follows his walk of life, finally got himself overmatched. I'll remember that about you, Mr. Willet."

"What do you want me to do now?" said Willet.

"Looks like justifiable self-protection," said the sheriff dryly. "You got yourself a witness."

"He sure has," said the desk clerk. "Bring on

122

your courts and prosecutors and stacks of Bibles. This man escaped only by the grace of God."

"Excuse me while I yawn," said the sheriff.

Willet said, "Sheriff Dorfmann, is there any way, any way at all, that I can get into the Recorder's office at the courthouse with someone that knows the books and look up some titles and deeds and such?"

"Not at this hour," said the sheriff kindly. "Not until nine tomorrow morning. What you got on your mind?"

"I don't know," said Willet. "And that's the heaven's truth. I don't know."

He walked with them to Main Street, said a restrained good night on separating from them, and headed for Parson Waterfield's.

Most of the shops along Main were already dark. Willet had gone maybe a block and a half when he came to a horse and buggy pulled up to the edge of the sidewalk before a still lighted bakery. A man was sitting in the buggy, drinking from a flat brownglass pint bottle and eating doughnuts. The combination sickened Willet. Then he took a good look at the man, skinny, potbellied, in a dirty doeskin tunic deep-fringed around the neckline. "Why Mr. Morgenson," said Willet. "Whatever brings you out of Aspen Creek all the way up here to Winslow?"

"Bless my soul, it's the gun tramp," said Morgenson, all amiability. "Care for a nice sugared doughnut and a sip of whiskey?"

"I don't believe so, thank you," said Willet. "Though it sounds mighty tasty. What did you say brought you here?"

"These things," said Morgenson, patting two parcels on the seat beside him.

"They must be interesting," said Willet.

"They are," said Morgenson. "This here is a black lace Spanish shawl, and this one is a spanking new white Stetson."

"They sound attractive," said Willet. "I'm in a kind of hurry, but not that much of a hurry, if you'd care to put them on for me."

"They ain't *mine,*" said Morgenson. "I'm delivering them as presents."

"I'd sure like to know who to," said Willet. "You don't often run into a fellow in a Stetson and a lace shawl."

"These are for two different people," said Morgenson patiently. "A lady *and* a gentleman. They're gifts for Tom Lustrell and Miss Lee. To try to make up for saying that it wouldn't be convenient to grant that little favor they asked. I don't know what got into me. I'll be glad to do what they asked. Tom and me is the same as blood brothers."

"What if I was to tell you that you were too late?" said Willet. "That they was scatter-gunned down through their window just a little while ago."

"I wouldn't believe it," exclaimed Morgenson. "Was they?"

"No. But what if I was to say so?"

"I'd be brokenhearted," said Morgenson.

"You'd be standing there beholding the dregs and skim of what was once a human being. You'd be looking at a man with all the joy and light gone out of his life."

"Listen, Mr. Morgenson," said Willet. "Why don't you pick up them reins and drive right back to Aspen Creek? Maybe Mr. Lustrell won't want to see you in spite of the wonderful gifts. You turned him down when he needed you."

"Oh, he'll want to see me, all right," said Morgenson smugly. "We give and take with each other. He forgives me my trespasses and I forgive him his."

Willet walked away.

He didn't want his contempt to show.

The parsonage stood next to a doll-sized steepled church, separated from it by a vacant lot, joined to it by a grape arbored path at the rear of the lot. Willet was no expert in parsonages, but it seemed to him Mr. Meacham hadn't been far off when he called it a hencoop. It was oblong, of unseasoned, white painted, thin lumber of the cheapest possible construction. Willet wouldn't wanted to have bet that Parson Waterfield himself hadn't put it up, that it wasn't part of his employment stipulation. Honey lamplight came from the front window. Inside, a child was having a tough wrassle practicing on a flute. The sacred musical instrument was the organ, of course. Every church congregation had members, old-timers, who considered not only fiddles but pianos as baubles of the devil. Even these fire and brimstoners, Willet had heard, would tolerate a little flute, if it was religious. Many music-loving preachers, sick to their gullets with organs, in their homes became magnificent flutists. This kid had a long way to go, though. Willet knocked.

A women in a drab dress and a polka dot apron, with a kind, tough face, who looked as though she should be holding a Sharps against Chiricahuas, said, "I'm Mrs. Waterfield. Did you wish to see the Reverend?"

"If he ain't busy," said Willet, respecting her profoundly, watching his manners carefully.

"Are you a lost soul?" she asked.

"I don't think so, ma'am," he said. "But I wouldn't want to say for sure."

"That really ain't in my territory, it's Preacher's," she said apologetically. "Come in."

He stepped inside.

There were three little girls in the room, two little boys, and a baby in a homemade pine cradle. It was one of the little girls who was tangling with the flute, and it was almost as big as she was. Parson Waterfield, small and tanned and knobby, with those hard eyes of his—eyes that had seen too many young unwed desperate mothers, too many chewed-off ears, too many starving bedbug-bitten infants—sat at a desk cater-cornered at the other end of the room, his framed notary license on the wall above him. Mrs. Waterfield hustled her brood together, took up the baby, said, "You're in good hands, son," and got them all through a door at the back.

After a moment's serene inspection of his visitor, Parson Waterfield said, "Sit down, Mr. Willet. Is this a religious call or a materialistic call? The former, I hope."

"You remember me from the Great Northern bar?" said Willet.

"Yes," said the parson. "And I hear a little gossip about you, too. I've heard they's some in town anxious to count coup on you."

"It's the Lustrells I'm worried about, father and daughter," said Willet. "Could you see your way to giving me a little information, and maybe helping them?"

"I was put on earth to help," said Parson Waterfield. "But they's a law over at Helena against a notary giving confidential information."

"Do you do quite a little of Murray Parrish's notary work?"

"About all of it, I'd say."

He hadn't yet heard of Parrish's death, or this was the time he would have said so.

"Am I wasting my time here?" asked Willet.

"We don't know yet," said Parson Waterfield tranquilly. "Let's talk a little more and find out."

"I'm going to put some questions to you," said Willet. "If you don't choose to answer, I can find out my answers tomorrow morning at the Recorder's office at the courthouse. Does

Murray Parrish own the Judith River Café?"

"No."

"The Great Northern Hotel?"

"No."

"The *Double Star* ranch?"

"No. He bought each of them. But he transferred them."

"Bought them with his own money?"

"No, I'd say."

"Who did he transfer them to?" asked Willet.

"He transferred them to a company."

"Don't tell me to a company called the Judith River Café Company," said Willet. "I couldn't stand it."

"To a company called the Little Belt Grazing and Mercantile Company," said the parson. "And that company is owned by just one man."

"How did that Mercantile get in there with that Grazing?" asked Willet.

"This man's a great expander and grabber," said Parson Waterfield. "I'd say he's got plans for the town here. I got a feeling he thinks he's just getting started."

"And that's as far as you care to go?" said Willet. "You wouldn't care to name him for me?"

"If I named him to you, I'd be breaking my trust to my notary office," said the parson. "And that means Sunday short-ribs to my wife and children. But my license don't say I can't show him to you. He'll be through that front door in about four minutes."

Willet went icy.

He said very softly, "Why did you tell me this, sir?"

"Because maybe I'm a coup-counter myself, in my own way," said Parson Waterfield. "Maybe I'm on your side, the righteous side."

"Righteous!" said Willet. "I've been called cactus-mean, but I never been called righteous before."

"He works in mysterious ways, His wonders to perform," said the parson. "When this man comes in he'll ask me for a document and I'll give it to him. You'd be interested in looking that document over, but I doubt if he'd be overjoyed at giving you the chance."

The front door opened and Julian Craycroft, the *Box L* foreman-manager, came in.

He came in striding arrogantly, with his face set in that tight-mouthed self-important way.

His eyes showed surprise at the sight of Willet, then hatred, then ignored Willet completely.

Walking to the desk, speaking, he said, "I'll have that you-know-what."

Parson Waterfield opened a drawer, took out a brown envelope, and handed it to him.

Craycroft said, "Mr. Parrish get in to sign it?"

"Not yet," said the parson.

"Then he won't be," said Willet. "I just had to kill him."

Craycroft went iron stiff.

Parson Waterfield's eyes showed a funny cloudy sort of satisfaction.

Willet said courteously, almost tenderly, "Mr. Craycroft, I wonder could I take a look inside that brown envelope you got there, the one you're holding so tight?"

Craycroft swiveled his head a quarter turn on his stiff neck, and looked at Willet.

It was the kind of look that Willet had seen before, the kind that always bothered him. It was a look made up of a mixture of fear, and desperation, and crazy fury. If a man with a look like that pulled his gun, he left this world in slavering frenzy while he emptied it. Anybody and everybody could die, even the little girl with the flute if she should wander in.

But Willet said it, because he had to say it.

He said gently, "Will you give it to me, or am I going to have to take it off you later?"

Like when the blaze has flared out of a piece of burning tissue paper, and crinkles and shrivels, Craycroft became a different man, listless, almost lifeless. As in a dream, he handed Willet the envelope.

Willet opened it, and tooke out a printed legal form that read:

DEED
From
Murray Parrish
  To
The Little Belt Grazing and Mercantile Company
  Know All Men By These Presents: That
MURRAY PARRISH in consideration of One

Dollar ($1.00) and other good and valuable con-
siderations to him paid by THE LITTLE
BELT GRAZING AND MERCANTILE
COMPANY the receipt of which is hereby ac-
knowledged, do hereby GRANT, BARGAIN,
SELL AND CONVEY unto the said LITTLE
BELT GRAZING AND MERCANTILE
COMPANY the following described real estate
to-wit: The ranch known as the Box L, being the
same premises recorded in Vol. 12, Page 117 of
the Deed Records of Winslow County, Montana,
To Have and to Hold (and so on)

Willet refolded the paper, put it back in the
envelope, returned the envelope to Craycroft.

Even before Parrish had gone through the
motions of owning the ranch, a transfer had
been made out to Craycroft.

"I think they call that counting your
chickens before they're hatched," said Willet.

"What good did that do you?" asked
Craycroft, trying to rally up a little bluster.

"It explained Mr. Lustrell's waylaying at
Dakins Station," said Willet. "And cleared up
a few other details."

"Such as what?" asked Craycroft.

"Such as who was the one who had me
chain-whipped," said Willet.

There was a moment of silence. Craycroft
licked his lips. "What do you aim to do?" he
asked. "I'm no gunslinger. Anybody can take
me. Even Preacher here."

"Don't tempt me," said Parson Waterfield.

Craycroft said, "Can I go now?"

"Mighty good idea," said Willet.

At the door, Craycroft said, "I won't bear no grudge if you don't."

"That's nice," said Willet.

When the foreman had gone, and Willet was alone with the parson, he said, "Who come out ahead, him or me?"

"It has to be racing falsified assets," said Parson Waterfield.

"What are you talking about?" asked Willet.

"There was a man doing it in Denver, when me and my family were living there. It was in all the papers. Everybody was talking about it. This man started out as a grocer and ended up owning just about everything."

"You talking to yourself?"

"I'm not talking to anybody; I didn't say anything," said Parson Waterfield.

XII

"So now you understand racing falsified assets," said Mr. Robert Treadway.

It was the next evening, just after sundown, and they were sitting in the autumn dusk in the Lustrell sideyard under the winesap tree, on kitchen chairs in a little row, Mr. Treadway, Mr. Lustrell, Miss Lee, and Willet, because Mr. Treadway, a city man, found the country ozone enjoyable. Supper was just over and Mr. Treadway held a coconut bonbon in one hand, a chunky cigar butt in the other. A glass of dandelion wine was on the ground in the curled dead leaves by his shoe sole. He was pulsating with repletion and content. They stared at him with respect and affection. He had come to town midmorning, and looked them up right after he'd registered at the boarding house and got Willet's message.

When he had heard Willet's story about Craycroft, he'd spent the forenoon busily about town, asking certain businessmen certain questions.

"You certainly did us a favor," said Miss Lee.

"I did other people a favor, too," said Mr. Treadway. "These things have to be stamped out. I was glad to do it."

He rammed the bonbon into his mouth, pouched it in one side of his jaw, and said, "Craycroft was just getting started on what was actually the old warehouse swindle, as old as the hills. He might have figured it out for himself, or he might have got the idea somewhere. It's a hoary old trick, and the raced assets is a variation that works quicker and is supposed to mix you up more. The *Double Star* would borrow from the Judith River Café, and the cafe might borrow from the Great Northern Hotel, and the hotel might borrow from the ranch or from the café. This was the racing part, the shuttle, negotiating back and forth within itself. False invoices. False assets. False appraisals. All values scooted up, inflated. And always new property was added. Pyramided. That is part of the swindle, new property, new property, new property. You start off with a little balloon and blow it up into a big one."

"And then it goes bango on you," said Willet.

"Of course, but you've taken care of that in advance. You've salted away money in the meantime. Craycroft hadn't salted any away as yet. He was still blowing it up."

"That offer Mr. Parrish made to Papa to sell him the *Double Star?*" said Miss Lee.

"That wasn't serious," said Mr. Treadway. "It was just a red herring to mix you up a little."

"And nobody beat Craycroft up, like he came and showed us," said Willet.

"Noboby, I'd say," said Mr. Treadway. "He probably did that to himself. To clear himself. You people were beginning to worry him."

"And I bet he had a craving for that big-house at *Box L,*" said Willet. "To him, it would be the chief's wigwam."

"It was my letter, mainly, that made him want it," said Mr. Treadway.

"Will the law get him?" asked Miss Lee.

"Very likely," said Mr. Treadway. "You ranchers have your laws and we businessmen have ours. And we don't fiddle when they're meddled with."

"What's a warehouse swindle?" asked Willet.

"That's when a man borrows on, or insures, nonexistent goods or chattels or commodities in a warehouse."

"Oh," said Willet.

"It was quite a favorite game at one time," said Mr. Treadway. "Believe it or not, it has even been done in nonexistent warehouses. This Craycroft seems to have used it on everything. I bet he even used nonexistent *Double Star* cows. Miss Lustrell, how's the chance of a little more of that delicious dandelion wine?"

Miss Lee went into the house, returned with a decanter, and filled Mr. Treadway's glass.

He circled the glass toward each of them in a silent toast, drank, and said comfortably, "I can taste the balmy spring breezes that kissed those dandelions."

"And you can taste its powder-keg wallop, too, can't you?" said Mr. Lustrell in happy praise.

Mr. Treadway had turned out to be a stocky little man in crinkly new blue serge, with a gray suede vest. His voice was friendly, and he had a genial way of tilting his chin when he spoke to you, but if you gave him a second look you saw his eyes and face muscles always remained expressionless, even though you were dealing him cards, and he was saying, "I think I'll stand pat." Willet figured him to be a top-rater in his line of work.

"To get back to this morning's topic," said Mr. Treadway. "To the thing that brought me out here. I wanted to talk to you. When I wrote you, as I did some time back, I didn't much care to be answered by someone I never heard of, named Craycroft."

"Like I explained to you," said Willet. "Mr. Lustrell never got that letter." That was the letter Morgenson had spoken of.

"Now I'm a slaughtering and packing man," said Mr. Treadway. "My judgment and money is in slaughtering and packing. And if you'll forgive me, Mr. Lustrell, there's a lot about the meat business I know, and maybe you don't. Let me tell you a few of those things."

"I'd like to hear 'em," said Mr. Lustrell, annoyed but trying to sound reasonable.

"Last year, countrywide, the average family paid out between a tenth and a third of its food money for meat; did you know that?" said Mr. Treadway.

"No, I didn't," said Mr. Lustrell. "And I find it interesting."

"Up until a few years ago," said Mr. Treadway. "Every village and town and city was supplied by local slaughterers. Now a big amount comes from Chicago and St. Louis packers."

"I heard that's the way it was," said Mr. Lustrell.

"Packers sell entirely by grades," said Mr. Treadway. "By the way, small towns usually want second grade stuff."

Mr. Lustrell looked dour.

"Which brings me to prime beef," said Mr. Treadway. "The only kind of beef to raise is prime beef."

"I know that," said Mr. Lustrell.

"You maybe only know part of it," said Mr. Treadway. "Let me tell you, from the packers' viewpoint. The packers want mature beef, because the younger stuff doesn't marble as well. And the distribution of fat in the muscles is one mark of high quality. The best flavor is in muscles that are frequently used. But those muscles are tough. So packers ripen even prime beef, keep it hanging in cold storage ten days or two weeks. All these things the man that raises the cows should completely understand."

"I always thought a steak right off the cow was best," said Willet.

"Well, it isn't," said Mr. Treadway. "Even from the best of steers. A high percentage of beef blood is valuable in the hanging. Mongrels don't have it. A prime steer has a surface coating of fat, which protects the lean beneath from exposure in the ripening. Medium and common grades sometimes don't have this surface fat, and low grades will actually rot in ripening. Cheaper cuts from prime beef are often better than the best cuts from low-grade stuff. It's only partly the cuts, you see; it's mainly the grade of beef. There's a higher percentage of dressed meat, too, in a prime steer, properly fatted. As you mighty well know, slaughters and packers pay a generous premium for this top-grade stuff."

"So what?" said Mr. Lustrell.

"So why raise any other kind? Why not keep weeding out all runts and culls and big jaws and the poor stuff as they go along?"

"I try to," said Mr. Lustrell.

"Try to how hard?" said Mr. Treadway. "Now here's my proposition again. I've got a few friends back in St. Louis with a little floating money, enough to buy a lot of good Texas yearlings. I was all over this country scouting last year. You've got some wonderful grass you don't seem to be much using. We'll put the feeders on your grass, and you'll raise them, fifty-fifty, even-steven?"

"I'll have to think it over," said Mr. Lustrell.

"He's thought it over," said Willet. "His answer is yes."

"Don't rush me," said Mr. Lustrell.

"Papa," said Miss Lee, in a strained numb voice, "I feel it coming over me that I'm going to lose my temper."

"It sounds like a fine proposition," said Mr. Lustrell hurriedly. "Thank you. I accept."

"I got the agreement papers right here," said Mr. Treadway. "Let's go in where's there some lamplight, and sign them."

To Willet, Mr. Lustrell said, "How would you like to be the new foreman of *Box L.*?"

"I'm just a drifter," said Willet.

"You could handle it, couldn't you?" asked Mr. Lustrell.

"If I couldn't, I'd shoot myself," said Willet. "I was born in a drywash, and thought I was a calf until they caught me in a roundup."

"Then you'll take it?" said Mr. Lustrell.

"He'll take it," said Miss Lee.

Merle Constiner was born in Monroe, Ohio. Other than the years he spent at Vanderbilt University, earning a Master's degree in Journalism, he lived his whole life in Monroe. It wasn't until the 1940s that he began publishing detective fiction extensively in pulp magazines like *Black Mask* and *Dime Detective Magazine*. In the 1950s he began contributing fiction to such slick magazines as *The Saturday Evening Post* and *The American Magazine*. It was first at the end of the decade that he published two original paperback Westerns, *Last Stand at Anvil Pass* (Fawcett, 1957) and *The Fourth Gunman* (Ace, 1958). Yet it wasn't until the 1960s, beginning with *Short-Trigger Man* (Ace, 1964), that Constiner came to specialize in Western fiction, producing a body of work that not only established his reputation but continues to retain its popularity with readers. He wrote in a simple, straightforward manner and populated his stories with unusual and memorable characters. *Death Waits at Dakins Station* (Ace, 1970) is both characteristic and typical of Constiner at his best, the story of an unemployed cowpuncher who is hired to take a message to Dakins Station and as a result finds himself in a complex intrigue. The ironic humor with which the story is told in this and his other books comprises the charm of his style. Constiner always attends to historical detail, geographic as well as social, and however conventional a situation may seem at first, his protagonists do not react quite like any others in Western fiction, an attribute of his Western stories that never allows them to lose their attraction and interest.